BY CELIA BARKER LOTTRIDGE

Ticket to Curlew

Wings to Fly

The Wind Wagon

BERTA
A REMARKABLE DOG

BERTA
A REMARKABLE DOG

CELIA BARKER LOTTRIDGE

WITH PICTURES BY
Elsa Myotte

A GROUNDWOOD BOOK
DOUGLAS & McINTYRE
TORONTO VANCOUVER BUFFALO

Groundwood Books/Douglas & McIntyre
720 Bathurst Street, Suite 500, Toronto, Ontario M5S 2R4

Distributed in the USA by Publishers Group West
1700 Fourth Street, Berkeley, CA 94710

We acknowledge the support of the Canada Council for the Arts, the
Ontario Arts Council and the Government of Canada through the Book
Publishing Industry Development Program for our publishing activities.

ONTARIO ARTS COUNCIL
CONSEIL DES ARTS DE L'ONTARIO

National Library of Canada Cataloguing in Publication Data
Lottridge, Celia B. (Celia Barker)
Berta : a remarkable dog
ISBN 0-88899-461-3 (bound). ISBN 0-88899-469-9 (pbk.)
I. Myotte, Elsa II. Title.
PS8573.O855B47 2002   jC813'.54   C2001-903209-9
PZ7.L918Be 2002

Design by Michael Solomon
Printed and bound in Canada

To Lucy and Jonathan

and the dogs we have known

Table of Contents

Chapter 1 : A REMARKABLE DOG : 11

Chapter 2 : A BOX OF CHICKS : 15

Chapter 3 : BEWARE THE PIG : 25

Chapter 4 : A KIDNAPPING : 31

Chapter 5 : A KNOCK ON THE DOOR : 40

Chapter 6 : BERTA'S BABY : 52

Chapter 7 : A BIG JOB : 62

Chapter 8 : GROWING : 72

Chapter 9 : PATRICK SPEAKS : 81

Chapter 10 : BERTA'S BABIES : 92

Berta lived in the small town of Middle Westfield in a yellow house with a barn behind it. She was a dog. A very remarkable dog. Most people who knew her thought she was quite ordinary, but they were wrong. The day would come when Berta would do something surprising. Something remarkable.

Berta was a sturdy dog with smooth brown fur. She had a long pointed nose and floppy ears. She also had very short legs.

"She looks like a sausage," said Rosalind

Mahoney who lived next door to the yellow house. "She's a sausage dog."

"No, she isn't," said Marjory Miller. Marjory was part of Berta's family. She was nine years old and Rosalind was her best friend. "I have told you at least fifty times. Berta is a dachshund. Dachshunds are supposed to have short legs. They were bred to hunt badgers. They can dig very fast and corner the badgers underground, in holes. If they had long legs they could never do that."

The dog they were discussing was curled in a doughnut shape on Marjory's bed. Her eyes were closed.

Rosalind looked at her.

"Berta would never be bothered to dig holes and go into them for any reason," she said. "She's too lazy. If any badgers lived in Middle Westfield they wouldn't have to worry."

Marjory had to agree that Berta was not a very energetic dog. Her favorite pastimes were eating and sleeping and, if necessary, taking short walks. Certainly not hunting. Other animals didn't interest her at all. If a neighborhood kitten pounced on her tail while she was resting under the lilac bush Berta just closed her eyes. And she never bothered to go down to the little barn where Mr. Miller kept chickens and pigs and the occasional calf.

"Maybe Berta doesn't want to hunt," Marjory said, "but when she does want something she is very determined. For instance, she knows perfectly well that she is not supposed to be on my bed, but if you tried to move her right now she would make herself as heavy as a big stone."

Berta opened her eyes halfway and gave Rosalind a long look.

"Don't worry, Berta," Rosalind said

quickly. "I wouldn't dream of moving you."

Berta closed her eyes and Marjory smiled. This was a dog who always knew exactly what she wanted and she almost always got it without making a fuss. Marjory was the only person who noticed. Even her parents, who had known Berta since puppyhood, only said things like, "Thank goodness Berta is such a quiet dog. No trouble at all."

When Rosalind had gone home Marjory gave Berta a hug and a pat.

"Someday you'll show people how clever you are, won't you?" she said.

And Berta did. She was, after all, a very remarkable dog.

CHAPTER 2
A BOX OF CHICKS

It was March, a bothersome month in Middle Westfield. Not winter and not spring. Marjory was tired of wearing her fat winter jacket, but if she changed to a thinner one she got cold to the bone playing outside at recess.

Marjory's mother, who taught biology at the high school, said, "I know that Nature needs this wretched month for some reason, but why does it have to last such a long time?"

Even Berta seemed restless. She whined

at the door, took one look at the patchy snow in the yard and refused to go out. A few minutes later she was whining at the door again.

Only Mr. Miller enjoyed March. He ran the hardware store in Middle Westfield but even more than hardware, he loved farm animals. That is why he wanted to live in a very small town.

"In Middle Westfield I can have farm animals without the bother of a farm," he liked to say, and it was true. No one in town minded a flock of chickens, some ducks, a few pigs and maybe a calf or two. So the Millers lived in a house with a barn where Mr. Miller could keep his animals. In March he always looked forward to the arrival of some new ones in time for spring.

"I've ordered fifty baby chicks from the hatchery," he told Marjory one Saturday morning. "They'll arrive at the post office today. Do you want to come with me to get them?"

"Oh, yes," said Marjory. Every year it amazed her that boxes of chicks came to the post office just like any other packages. Of course, the boxes had holes punched all around the sides so that the chicks could breathe, and they were shallow so that the chicks would not pile up on top of each other. And they came express post so that the chicks would get to their new homes as soon as possible.

When Marjory and her dad walked into the post office they knew immediately that the chicks were there. They could hear them cheeping. The cheeping was surprisingly loud because many boxes of chicks had come in that day for all the people around Middle Westfield who raised chickens. There were big boxes with one hundred chicks and smaller ones with fifty.

The postmistress handed Mr. Miller one of the smaller boxes.

"You'll have to keep these fellows indoors for a while," she said. "Too cold for them outside right now."

"We've got a nice warm spot all ready," said Mr. Miller. He put the box in the back seat of the car and he and Marjory drove home.

The place reserved for the chicks was in the storeroom off the kitchen. As soon as her dad set the box on the floor Marjory lifted off the lid. There were fifty fuzzy yellow chicks huddled in the corners of the box.

"You must hate being shut up and moved around in the dark," Marjory said to them. "Don't worry, you're home now."

"They only hatched the day before yesterday," said Mr. Miller, "so they don't know what to expect. But I bet they'd like some food and water." He put chick mash in two bowls and water in two more and set them down in the box. Then he put a desk lamp beside the box, close enough for the bulb to keep the chicks warm.

"In a week or so they'll have some feathers and be big enough to move to the barn," he said. "This will keep them happy for now."

Marjory sat watching the chicks begin to walk around. Some found the mash and began pecking at it. She hoped they were happy. She picked one chick up and felt its little poky feet prickling the palm of her hand. When she put it down it cuddled into a corner with most of the others and went to sleep.

That's about all chicks did, she remembered. When they were cute they cheeped and slept. Then they turned into chickens. Marjory was not very fond of chickens.

She said good-bye to the chicks and went over to Rosalind's house.

At suppertime Mr. Miller looked in on the chicks before he sat down at the kitchen table.

"They're doing fine," he said. "I can almost believe they're bigger now than they were when we brought them home."

Berta was curled up beside the radiator in the corner. She always spent mealtimes in that spot pretending to be asleep. Marjory knew that she really was watching through her eyelashes, ready to get up quietly if a crust of bread or a strand of spaghetti landed on the floor. Berta did not let any food go to waste.

Tonight she saw Berta open her eyes and look at the family eating and talking. Then she got up but she didn't come to the table. Instead she walked stealthily, with her toenails clicking just a little on the tile, to the storeroom door. It was open a crack and Berta gently pushed at it with her nose until it opened just a little more. Then she disappeared through the opening.

Marjory stopped eating lasagna. Why would Berta want to go into the storeroom? Maybe she had heard the chicks and was investigating the sound. Well, thought Marjory, I had better investigate Berta.

She got up from the table and pushed the door wide open. There was the box of chicks with the light shining down on them. And there was Berta with her nose in among the chicks.

"What are you doing, Berta?" said Marjory. "Are you sniffing them? They're just baby chickens."

She looked more closely. Berta had her mouth open. Marjory could see her long pink tongue. Was she eating the chicks?

For a moment Marjory couldn't move

or make a sound. Then she saw that long pink tongue skimming over the heads of the chicks.

Berta was licking the chicks. She was doing her best to wash them, following them around the box with her nose and lapping at them with her tongue.

The chicks did not want to be washed. They were scrambling away from the large damp thing that had suddenly appeared above them but Berta would not give up.

Marjory found her voice.

"Berta, stop!" she said and grabbed her dog by the collar. She pulled her out of the storeroom and shut the door firmly. Berta gave her a resentful look and went back to the radiator where she curled up with her back to the room.

"What was all that about? Was Berta doing something to the chicks?" said Mrs. Miller.

"She was licking them," said Marjory. "She didn't hurt them. They just got a little wet. But why would she want to lick those fuzzy things? She never did before."

"I don't know," said Mrs. Miller, "but we'd better keep the storeroom door shut tight. Berta might drown a chick with that big tongue of hers."

But Berta didn't even look at the storeroom door after that, as far as Marjory could tell.

"Probably she was just curious," she said to herself. But she wondered.

CHAPTER 3
BEWARE THE PIG

The chicks were still living in the storeroom when Mr. Miller burst through the back door early the next Saturday morning with a wide grin on his face.

"Great news," he said to his sleepy family. "We have six new baby pigs. Born last night. Prettiest piglets you ever saw."

Marjory smiled back at her dad. He thought pigs were the best of all animals. She liked them quite well, too, but she would never call them pretty. Still, baby pigs could certainly be called cute. She decided to visit them right after break-fast.

March was still being miserable so she put on her warm jacket even though the barn was only a two-minute walk away.

"Wear your old boots," said her mother. "It's so muddy around the barn."

Marjory picked her way across the muddy yard, shivering in the raw wind. She was glad to get into the shelter of the barn and pull the big door shut behind her. She loved the barn. It had three stalls downstairs and a loft above. Rosalind liked to say it was really an overgrown shed, but it felt like a barn and it smelled of clean and well-fed animals. The air was strangely warm.

Dad said that was because of the pigs.

"They used to build animal sheds right next to the farm houses just for the warmth," he told her.

Marjory liked to imagine a house with a pig standing patiently in each room in place of a radiator, giving off heat.

It would be smelly but interesting, she decided. But the pigs would probably get bored.

Right now two of the stalls were empty and one was full of the mother pig and her six piglets. Marjory leaned on the railing and smiled at the sight of them. She had forgotten how big the mother pig was and how small the piglets would look next to her. They were Hampshire pigs, which meant they were black with neat belts of white around their middles. The mother pig lay on her side like a mountain with all the babies neatly lined up along her belly, nursing.

It was very quiet. Marjory could hear the piglets snuffle a little as they sucked, but the mother seemed to be asleep.

Then she heard another sound, like very quiet footsteps.

There was cold air blowing into the barn. The door had come open. And something was pushing against Marjory's ankles.

She looked down.

"Berta," she said. "What are you doing? You never come into the barn."

Berta paid no attention. She was beside Marjory, sticking her nose between the slats of the stall railing. She seemed to be trying to push herself right into the stall.

The mother pig lifted her head. Her little shiny eyes looked straight at Berta. Her ears twitched and a sound like the creaking of a rusty hinge came from her throat.

Marjory grabbed Berta's collar and pulled hard.

"Berta, you can't go in there. That pig is getting mad," she said sharply.

She pulled until even the tip of Berta's

nose was safely outside the railing. Then she took a quick look into the pen, without letting go of the collar.

The mother pig had laid her head back down, but her eyes were open and watchful. The piglets were still lying peacefully in their row, sucking.

"Come on, Berta," said Marjory firmly. "You don't belong in the barn. Remember, you're a house dog."

Berta trotted ahead of her out the open door. "You're getting too good at opening doors," Marjory said and led the way back to the house.

At dinner that night she told her parents all about it. Her dad shook his head.

"Pigs are fierce mothers," he said. "Berta had better stay away from the barn."

"I know," said Marjory. She imagined Berta squashed flat under a huge mother pig. "I'll keep my eye on her."

"I wonder what has gotten into our quiet dog?" said Mrs. Miller. "She's always liked comfort above everything. Why is she interested in the pigs all of a sudden? It's just not like her."

Marjory remembered the chicks. That was strange, too. She looked at Berta who was curled up in her usual spot. She wasn't even pretending to be asleep. She was watching Marjory. Then she winked.

"But dogs don't wink," Marjory told herself.

She wondered what would happen next.

Marjory was walking slowly home from school. Rosalind had a dentist appointment so she was all alone. It was a nice day for a walk. The sky was blue and the air was almost warm. It was easy to think that spring was near, but Marjory knew that it really wouldn't come until sometime in April, and April was still weeks away.

She was just crossing the street in front of her house when she saw Berta running across the yard.

Marjory stopped and stared. Berta never

ran unless someone was holding something very delicious and calling her. But there was no one in sight.

And where was Berta going? She wasn't heading for the back door, and she was paying no attention to Marjory. She was running around to the front of the house with her head down, as if she was hiding something.

Sneaky, thought Marjory. That's how she looks. Sneaky.

Marjory began to run, too. She cut across the yard hoping to catch Berta before she disappeared. She seemed to be heading for the space under the front porch where old flower pots were stored.

"Stop, Berta," she called, but she knew it was useless. Berta was not going to stop. She was determined to do something that was either very important to her or very bad. Or maybe both.

Marjory dropped her books and grabbed Berta around the middle with both hands just as she was about to disappear under the porch.

"What are you doing, you silly dog?" she said. She sat down on the bottom step and held Berta by the collar so that she could look her in the eye.

But Berta wouldn't look at her.

"It's okay. I won't get mad. What's the matter?" But Berta kept her chin down and her head twisted away.

"I know what it is," said Marjory, getting a little cross. "You have something you're not supposed to have. Maybe something really yucky. Well, I have to see it."

She put one hand under Berta's chin and Berta suddenly looked up.

There, sticking out of her mouth, was a tail. A little spiky tail with black fur.

"Oh, Berta," Marjory whispered. "You

can't have a whole animal in your mouth.
You just can't." But she knew that Berta
could. And did.

Berta blinked but she did not open her
mouth.

Marjory drew a deep breath.

"Drop it, Berta," she said quietly but
very firmly. "Drop it!" And even though she
did not know what might fall out of Berta's
mouth, she kept one hand under her chin.

Berta slowly opened her mouth and a
tiny kitten fell out into Marjory's hand. It
was curled up so that she couldn't see
whether it was hurt, but its black fur was
damp and it wasn't moving at all.

She let go of Berta's collar and held the
kitten in both hands. Even though she was
worried about what she might see, she
looked the kitten over as well as she could
without moving it around. It was so young
that its eyes weren't open.

"Oh, please. Be alive," whispered Marjory. "Please be alive."

The kitten lay perfectly still for an endless moment. Then it opened its mouth very wide and gave a tiny squeaking *meew*.

"Thank goodness," said Marjory. She could breathe again. She looked at Berta who was staring at the kitten in her hands. "Why did you steal a kitten, Berta? And what were you going to do with it? I wish you could talk."

She got up, leaving her books lying on the ground. "Come on, Berta. We've got to tell Mom what you've brought home."

Her mother was sitting at the kitchen table marking papers but she got up and opened the door when she heard Marjory calling.

"What do you have there?" she asked. "Is something wrong?"

Marjory held out her cupped hands so

that her mother could see what she was carrying.

"A kitten," said Mrs. Miller. "Where on earth did you find such a tiny one? It should be with its mother."

"It wasn't me," said Marjory. "It was Berta. She kidnapped this kitten. She brought it home in her mouth and I saw its tail sticking out. Oh, Mom, I was so scared it would be dead."

Mrs. Miller took the kitten from her gently and looked it over carefully.

"It looks fine," she said, "but it does need to get back to its mother."

"Probably it belongs to one of Jenny Jefferson's cats. There are always kittens in her shed. I'll take it over there," said Marjory. "But, Mom, why would Berta steal a kitten? She's being so strange. Why would she want to get into the pig pen? And why would she lick the chicks?"

Mrs. Miller looked at Berta who was sitting beside her staring longingly up at the kitten.

"I guess it's babies," she said. "Berta has never had puppies and she probably feels it's time. I'm sorry, Berta. There are so many animals around this place in the spring that I don't want puppies, too. In the fall we can find a nice father for your pups. Wouldn't you like to have puppies in the fall?"

"Poor Berta," said Marjory. "How can she understand?"

She got a soft cloth to make a nest for the kitten and carried it over to Jenny Jefferson's house. Jenny was a tiny gray-haired woman who cared for cats above all else. She had five of her own, fed many more and always found good homes for the kittens that were born in her shed.

She looked at the black kitten and said, "Why that's one of Midnight's litter. You say your dog stole it? Must be a very gentle dog. The kitten is fine but you keep that dog away."

"We will," said Marjory. "She has never done such a thing before. Will Midnight take the kitten back?"

"I'm going to rub it all over with a towel the kittens have been sleeping on," said Jenny. "That should do the trick. Midnight is a good mother. She'll take it back."

Marjory walked home feeling sorry for Berta. She had carried that kitten home so gently, just because she wanted babies of her own.

I'll let her sleep on my bed tonight, she decided. And I'll tell her that next fall isn't so far away. If only she could understand.

CHAPTER 5

A KNOCK ON THE DOOR

By the next Saturday every hint of spring was gone. The sky was gray and the wind whipped scraps of sleet against the windows.

"At least it's not a school day," said Rosalind. "I don't mind walking as far as your house on a day like this, but school? No thank you."

Marjory agreed. It was a day to stay home. She and Rosalind had spent the morning making chocolate chip cookies. Berta was upstairs, probably sleeping on

Marjory's bed. She knew from experience that nobody ever gave her treats when they were baking, so she didn't bother to hang about hoping for handouts.

Now all the cookies were baked and the girls were cleaning up the flour that had somehow spread itself evenly over every flat surface in the kitchen. Marjory stopped to admire the rows of enticing brown cookies cooling on the racks. Not even one was burned and they had taken care of the few broken ones by eating them.

Her mother came into the kitchen and said, "Those are gorgeous cookies and the smell is driving me crazy but let's don't eat any till after lunch. I have some chili in the fridge. You girls can peel carrots for carrot sticks. And of course dessert is just waiting there, thanks to you."

In two minutes the table was set and the chili was warming on the stove.

Just then there was a knock at the back door.

"Would you see who that is, Rosalind?" said Mrs. Miller, who was stirring the chili. "I'm not expecting anyone but there's plenty of food."

Rosalind opened the door and a man stepped into the kitchen. The wind banged the storm door behind him and he stood wiping his boots on the mat.

"This is some terrible day," he said. He was wearing a hat with earflaps and a plaid wool jacket. Marjory thought that he was carrying something inside the jacket, holding it against his chest as if it needed protecting.

"Why, it's Jack Steiner, isn't it," said Mrs. Miller. "I didn't recognize you at first in that hat. What brings you to town?"

"Well, I wouldn't have come if I didn't have a problem," said Mr. Steiner. "You know I raise sheep and it's lambing time. Not a good time to be away but my wife said she could look after things for a couple of hours and I have this little fellow to worry about."

"What little fellow?' said Marjory.

"He's right here," said Mr. Steiner, patting the left side of his jacket. "I had to keep him out of the wind. He was just born this morning, you know."

Marjory started to speak but her mother said, "Tell us about him."

"I have this ewe," said Mr. Steiner. "She's a good mother but cranky and she had twins this time, both fine healthy lambs. But she only wants to take care of one of them. She'll have nothing to do with this one, though he's big and healthy."

He stopped talking and looked around the kitchen. "I guess your husband isn't home?"

"No, he's down at the store," said Mrs. Miller. Suddenly she smiled. "Now I understand. You have a lamb that needs a home and Tom always likes to give a home to a baby farm animal."

"Well, yes," said Mr. Steiner. "I thought you folks might like to have a lamb to raise. He has to be fed with a bottle and I just don't have the time and I know Tom Miller would take good care of him."

"Please, could we see him?" said Marjory. She didn't know whether her mom would want a lamb, but surely if she saw him she couldn't resist.

Jack Steiner unbuttoned his jacket and took out a bundle wrapped in a green towel. He set it on a chair and carefully folded back the cloth.

Marjory and Rosalind came close and saw a small heap of grayish white wool and a little face with a black nose and black eyes blinking in the light of the kitchen.

"Easy, little guy," said Mr. Steiner.

"Can I hold him?" asked Marjory.

"Sure you can. Sit down and I'll put him in your lap."

The lamb felt solid and warm even through the towel. Marjory and Rosalind gently touched his wool, and he shivered his skin as if he liked being touched.

Mrs. Miller watched for a moment and then said, "I'd say the decision is made as long as you girls promise to help with the feeding. I have a feeling that lambs like to eat often."

"You're right about that," said Jack Steiner. "Every two hours the first week, I'm afraid. Then every four hours for a week. Aside from that, lambs are pretty sturdy. Just keep him warm till he's put on a little weight."

"But what do we feed him?" asked Mrs. Miller.

"Glad you asked," said the farmer. "I almost forgot. I brought you some ewe's milk to start him out on. When that's gone just give him regular cow's milk. And I brought you some special nipples to feed him with. Just put one on a pop bottle. I'll get them from the truck and then I'd better get back. There will be some new lambs to look after when I get home, I expect. Oh, by the way, I raise these lambs for wool. If you don't want to shear him just bring him back to me."

When he was gone Mrs. Miller said, "It's a good thing for this lamb that I said yes before I heard about feeding him every two hours." Rosalind laughed but Marjory hardly heard. She was looking at the small animal lying in her lap.

"A lamb," she said. "When I woke up

this morning I didn't know we would have a lamb by lunchtime."

"Speaking of lunch, I'd better find a box to put your new friend in. I don't think you can eat and hold a lamb in your lap at the same time."

Mrs. Miller hurried off and came back with a square cardboard box with an old blanket in it. She set it in the warmest corner of the room, the one where Berta always napped. Then she picked up the lamb and put him in the box. He lay there looking suddenly very small and lonely.

"We should give him a name," said Marjory. "Maybe he'll feel more at home when we know what to call him. But what's a good name for a lamb?"

"I know the perfect name," said Rosalind. "Today is the seventeenth of March. St. Patrick's Day. Notice my green socks. Anyway, I think you should name him Patrick since St. Patrick's Day is his birthday."

"Patrick," said Marjory, trying it out. "Patrick. I think it's a good name."

"So do I," said her mother.

But Patrick the lamb still looked small and lonely.

I can't hold him on my lap all the time, thought Marjory. But what else can I do to make him feel at home?

Then the door opened. Not the back door but the door into the living room. It was shut to keep the kitchen warm and cozy. Now it creaked open and Berta walked in.

Everyone stared at her, all thinking the same thing.

What would Berta think of Patrick? What would she do?

Berta looked at Marjory, who usually

greeted her with a pat, but Marjory didn't move or speak. Then she looked around the room and saw the box. She stood still looking at this strange object sitting in her special warm spot. Then, without hurrying, she walked right over to see exactly what it was.

She looked over the edge of the box, stretching her neck just a little.

There was Patrick the lamb looking back at her.

For a moment Berta and Patrick just looked at each other.

Then Berta jumped. With one smooth motion she was over the side of the box and standing beside Patrick. She sniffed him carefully from head to tail and seemed satisfied. Then she lay down and curled herself around him. When she was nicely settled she raised her head and looked at Mrs. Miller and Marjory and Rosalind.

"She isn't going to move," said Marjory.

"She looks totally determined," said Rosalind.

"I know what it is," said Mrs. Miller. "Berta has found herself a baby."

The instant Marjory heard her mother say, "Berta has found herself a baby," she knew that it was true. Berta was exactly where she wanted to be, curled protectively around Patrick, who was looking much larger as Berta's baby than he had as a lonely lamb. Berta lay perfectly still, but her eyes were alert, watching the three people standing around her.

"Berta is a dog," said Rosalind. "How can she be a mother to a lamb? Anyway, she's too small. Patrick is a baby but he's already taller than Berta. You'll see as soon as he stands up."

"That doesn't matter," said Marjory. "Berta is determined and she knows Patrick needs her. She'll figure out what to do."

"And we'll help her," said Mrs. Miller. "We'll have to do the feeding, for one thing. No matter how determined she is, Berta can't produce milk for a lamb."

Just then Berta lifted her head and gave a sort of whining yelp. When nothing happened she yelped again.

Marjory said, "What do you want, Berta?"

Berta uncurled herself and sat up on her haunches. She looked at Patrick who was moving restlessly beside her. Then she yelped louder.

Mrs. Miller looked at her watch.

"Oh," she said. "It must be time to feed this lamb. I suppose it's been about two hours since he left the farm. Are you hungry, Patrick?"

She went to the refrigerator and got out the bottle of milk Jack Steiner had left.

"How did Berta know?" asked Rosalind.

"Maybe she could feel him getting restless, or maybe she could hear his stomach growling," said Mrs. Miller.

"Maybe she just knows these things now that she's his mother," said Marjory.

"Don't go thinking mothers know everything," said Mrs. Miller. "But right now I know that Patrick isn't the only one who needs feeding. You serve up the chili, Marjory, and I'll get Patrick started."

She warmed some of the milk, poured it into a big pop bottle and snapped on the extra long nipple. When she held it out to Patrick, he began to suck on it greedily. Berta lay down, but she didn't take her eyes off Patrick and the bottle.

They spent lunchtime taking turns holding the bottle and eating their chili. By the time they got to the cookies, Patrick and Berta were both asleep, curled up together.

All afternoon Marjory resisted the temptation to call her father and tell him about Patrick. It was hard, but she decided that it was too good a surprise to ruin. At six o'clock she volunteered to set the table so that she would be on hand when he came in the door.

"Tom never gets home till twenty past. How long can you spend setting the table?" teased her mother.

Marjory didn't answer, but she had never set the table so carefully. She folded the napkins into triangles and lined up the knives, forks and spoons perfectly. She even found some green candles in the back of a cupboard and made a St. Patrick's Day centerpiece.

She was just thinking about drawing a picture to decorate each place when the back door opened.

"What's this? A party? Is it somebody's birthday?" said her father.

"Actually it is," said Marjory. "Somebody you've never met, but he's come to live with us. Look." She led him over to the box.

Mr. Miller looked down at Patrick.

"A lamb? What is a lamb doing in our kitchen?" he said. "I'm sure he wasn't here when I left home this morning. And what is Berta doing in there with him? Did she find a lamb to bring home this time?"

While he took off his coat and boots Marjory told him the whole story.

"And Berta has adopted him. She's decided to be his mother," she finished up.

"I don't suppose Berta will take on all

the responsibility," said her father. "What do we know about feeding this baby?"

"He has to eat every two hours for the first week. But I'll help. I'll take my turn."

"Not in the night," said her mother. "You need your sleep. Anyway, Tom and I have had experience getting up to feed a baby. We'll do the night shift."

And her father said the same thing when it was bedtime.

"You have to understand that I've always wanted to raise a lamb. I look forward to getting up at midnight and two o'clock and four o'clock and six."

"I'll get up at two," said her mother. "That's not so bad."

"I can do the six o'clock one," said Marjory. "I almost get up at six anyway."

"Six in the morning is quite different than seven," said her father. "But set your alarm. I'll be glad not to get up at six."

So Marjory set her alarm and fell asleep reminding herself that it was her responsibility to actually wake up when it went off. There was a baby to be fed.

She dreamed about sheep all night, and about Berta who had grown large and was herding many sheep into the barn. One little one kept wandering off and Berta ran after it, barking. The barking got louder and louder until Marjory opened her eyes.

The room was very dark and the barking didn't stop. It wasn't part of her dream any more. She fumbled for her lamp switch. When the light came on, the room was suddenly quiet. Marjory, squinting in the brightness, saw Berta beside the bed, staring at her and then looking at the door.

Suddenly Marjory remembered. Patrick. She was supposed to feed Patrick. Her clock said 6:15.

"Oh, Berta, I'm sorry. I didn't hear my

alarm. But I guess you did and then you had to wake me up."

Berta was not listening. She was going to the top of the stairs and coming back. It was clear that she wanted Marjory to hurry up. So Marjory hurried. She put on her slippers and bathrobe and went slowly down the stairs. She didn't feel very awake and she didn't want to stumble.

Patrick was waiting. He struggled to his feet when he heard them coming and looked over the side of the box. Marjory wanted to pick him up and hug him, but she didn't. She got out the bottle she and her mother had fixed the night before. She set it in a pan of warm water to take the chill off and then she offered it to Patrick.

He opened his mouth and closed it around the nipple and began to suck so hard that Marjory almost dropped the bottle. She sat down and got a better grip.

Berta lay next to her and watched Patrick eat.

When her parents came down an hour later they found Patrick and Berta curled up together in the box and Marjory lying sound asleep on the rug with the empty bottle in her hand.

She woke up when she smelled bacon and toast.

"It's hard to get up early when you're not used to it," she said at breakfast.

"I noticed that you needed two wake-up alarms," said her father. When she looked puzzled he went on. "First I heard your alarm clock ring for a long time and then I heard barking. I was sure the barking wouldn't stop until you woke up, so I just put my head under the pillow and went back to sleep."

"I didn't hear my alarm clock," said Marjory. "But I guess Berta did and she knew I was supposed to feed Patrick so she made sure I woke up."

"Remarkable for Berta to figure that out," said Mrs. Miller. "Very surprising."

Marjory just smiled and went on eating toast and jam. She was still sleepy but she wasn't surprised. Not at all.

CHAPTER 7
A BIG JOB

Taking care of Patrick was a big job for Berta. Marjory could see that. Having decided that Patrick was her baby, Berta settled down to look after him completely. She slept in the box with him, watched him anxiously when he took a few wobbly steps around the kitchen and breathed a sigh of relief when he was safely curled up beside her.

When she felt it was time for him to be fed she sat up in the box and gave one sharp yip. If no one came immediately with a bottle she got out of the box and stood by the refrigerator, barking occasionally until someone said, "Oh, yes, Berta. I know, it's time to feed the baby," and went and got the milk. Then she watched every move the person holding the bottle made. Marjory could imagine her saying, "You're holding the bottle too high." Or she might say to Patrick, "Don't be so greedy. There's plenty of milk."

Marjory loved to feed Patrick because he ate with so much enthusiasm. He stretched out his neck and braced his feet and sucked so hard she expected all the milk to disappear inside him in one long gulp. When he was finished he lay down looking completely satisfied and fell asleep immediately. Berta curled up beside him looking satisfied, too.

"You're a good mother, Berta," Marjory said to her. "Patrick is a lucky

lamb. You are the best mother he could have."

There was one problem. Berta, being a dog, felt that she should keep her baby clean by licking him. Patrick, being a lamb, was very hard to lick. He was not covered with nice smooth fur but with curly wool that was a bit oily. Dust stuck to it so that Patrick, though very cute, was pale gray instead of snowy white.

"I don't think ewes worry about keeping their lambs clean," said Mr. Miller. He and Marjory were watching Berta lick Patrick's back. She had to stand up to do it and she had been working from his shoulders back, licking and licking, for a long time. The part she had licked looked a little cleaner than the rest but there was a lot of Patrick still to wash. Marjory felt tired just watching her.

Finally Berta stopped. She lay down

beside Patrick and lay there with her eyes open and her tongue hanging out a little.

"She's thinking," said Marjory. "She's trying to decide how she can keep Patrick clean.

"I think it's a hopeless task," said her dad. "Lambs were not meant to be licked. You just have to let them get grubby. There's no other way."

The next day Marjory saw Berta licking Patrick again. She was lying beside him licking a spot on his shoulder that she could comfortably reach. After a while she stopped and Marjory went to see what she had accomplished.

There on Patrick's shoulder was a patch of fluffy white wool about the size of a playing card.

"Wow, Berta, you got him really clean in that spot," said Marjory. "When are you going to do the rest?"

But Berta never did. She had found a

way to keep a small part of Patrick as clean as she thought he should be. She was not going to try to do the impossible job of washing all of her large baby.

"I guess she thinks that we should do our part, too," Marjory told her dad. "We could try washing him."

"Well, I draw the line at washing a lamb," he answered. "I think Patrick looks very distinguished with that white mark on his shoulder. It shows that he is Berta's baby."

And that was the way it stayed. After three days Berta and Patrick had settled into a comfortable routine of eating and sleeping and a little bit of washing.

On the fourth day Marjory brought two friends home from school with her. One, of course, was Rosalind who had not seen Patrick since the day he arrived. The other was Russell Wilcox, a boy in their class who lived just down the street and had a scientific interest in animals. He had many pets including a white rat and a descented skunk, but he had never had a lamb. Naturally he wanted to meet Patrick.

The three of them came stomping and laughing into the kitchen and the door banged behind them.

Marjory was struggling with her jacket zipper when Russell said, "What's the matter with your dog?'

She looked up and saw Berta sitting up in the box with her teeth bared. Rosalind was still laughing so Marjory couldn't hear, but she was sure that Berta was growling. She opened her mouth to say, "We'd better quiet down. Berta is getting upset," but before she could speak Rosalind was kneeling beside the box.

"Oh, you adorable baby," she said and stuck out her hand to touch Patrick.

Berta opened her mouth and in a split second she had closed it on Rosalind's wrist. Marjory stared in horror waiting for Rosalind to yell or cry but she just sat without moving at all with her wrist between Berta's teeth. Russell was staring, too.

"She isn't actually biting you, is she?" he finally asked in a quiet voice.

"No," said Rosalind shakily. "She's just holding on. She won't let go."

Then Marjory could speak. "It's all right, Berta," she said. "Rosalind won't hurt Patrick. You can let go."

Berta turned her eyes around to look at Marjory and her forehead wrinkled up. She waited just a moment longer and then she opened her mouth a little.

Rosalind carefully slid her wrist out. Then she sat back on her heels and took a deep breath.

"Berta didn't like that, did she?" she said.

"I guess it's part of her job to protect Patrick," said Marjory.

"But she didn't think you were a serious threat," said Russell. "If she had she would have really bitten you."

"Thank goodness," said Rosalind. "But after all these years I should hope she would know I wouldn't hurt Patrick." She looked at Berta. "But I get the message. I'll never do it again. I promise."

After that they all sat quietly around the box and watched Patrick. They even patted him but they checked to make sure it was all right with Berta before they did.

Russell said, "Patrick is living a very unusual life for a lamb. He's in a house, not a barn. He's fed without having to scramble. And he has his own personal dog to protect him."

"And he has a mark on his shoulder to show how special he is," said Marjory, and she told them why Patrick had a white patch. "I guess it's all part of the job. Washing, protecting."

"And Patrick just thinks it's normal," said Rosalind. And they all laughed, but quietly.

CHAPTER 8
GROWING

Patrick grew. He grew very fast. He took up more and more space in his sleeping box and when he was on his feet he looked tall and wide, especially when he stood next to Berta.

None of this made any difference to Berta. She went right on curling up next to him in the box. She made sure he got fed and she licked the white spot on his shoulder every day.

Patrick didn't seem to notice that his mother was only half as tall as he was. He let Berta push him around in the box until he was lying the way she wanted him to, and he peacefully ate when she thought it was time. He paid no attention at all when she licked him. He was a perfectly contented lamb.

Marjory's mother did notice how much Patrick had grown. One day when he was two and a half weeks old she said, "It's April now and getting quite warm. I think Patrick and Berta could move to the side porch. The railing and the gate will keep Patrick from falling off the edge. It's time he had a chance to roam around a bit."

Marjory agreed that Patrick couldn't spend his whole life indoors, but she couldn't help thinking that the kitchen would seem a bit empty without him.

Mr. Miller chose a moment when Berta was out in the yard and Patrick was asleep to move their box. He simply picked it up with Patrick in it, carried it out the door and set it on the porch in a sunny corner.

Patrick didn't seem to mind at all. He lifted his head and looked around but he stayed in the box.

Marjory didn't want Patrick's devoted mother to come into the kitchen and find her baby gone, so she went outside and found Berta having a brief nap beside the lilac bush.

"Come on, Berta," she said. "Patrick has moved to the side porch. I'll show you. You'll both be fine there."

Berta came but she was not pleased. She jumped into the box to sniff Patrick. Then she jumped out again and went to the door. She whined and looked at Marjory.

"No, Berta," said Marjory. "This is where Patrick will live now. That's what Mom says and she's just as stubborn as you are."

Maybe Berta knew she couldn't win or maybe the thought of living with Patrick on the porch didn't really seem so terrible to her. She soon jumped back into the box and settled down by licking Patrick's white spot vigorously. When night came, she didn't bark to come inside. She snuggled up very close to Patrick and went to sleep.

Before bedtime Marjory and her dad went out to look at them in the light that shone through the living-room window. They looked as cozy as ever.

"Berta certainly chose the right baby for a cool night like this," said Mr. Miller. "Now it's Patrick's turn to keep his mother warm."

One week later Marjory came home from school and found Patrick looking over the porch gate while Berta slept. He seemed to be looking longingly at the green spring grass.

"Couldn't Patrick go out in the yard now?" she asked her mother. "I'll watch him. I think he's tired of the porch."

"I agree with you. It's time for him to be outdoors," said Mrs. Miller. "If he had stayed on the farm he'd be out in the pasture with his mother. And if he's in the yard he can start eating grass. You could put him out now and see how he likes it."

Marjory immediately phoned Rosalind and Russell. They had to be on hand for this important moment in Patrick's life.

They came right away. When they arrived, Patrick was still looking over the gate. Berta had woken up and was watching him from the box.

Rosalind opened the gate and Marjory lifted Patrick down the steps. She set him down in a spot where the grass was particularly green.

Before she could move away from Patrick, Berta was standing beside her.

"Amazing," said Russell. "That dog heard the gate open and jumped and instantly she was way over there. I didn't think a dachshund could move so fast."

"Berta, it's okay," said Marjory. But Berta paid no attention to her. She went right up to Patrick, who was standing quietly on the grass looking around. She butted her head against him, trying to push him toward the steps.

"No, Berta," said Marjory. "Leave Patrick alone. He's all right. He can't live in a box forever. It's okay."

She half pulled and half coaxed her reluctant dog over to the steps and sat down beside her. She put her hand on Berta's back to comfort her and felt her whining inside.

"Shhh," she said to her friends. When

she bent close she could hear those very quiet whines and she knew that Berta really did not like what was happening.

Patrick, on the other hand, didn't look at all bothered. He stood on the grass looking around. He seemed quite happy but not inclined to do anything.

"Marjory," said Russell suddenly. "Has Patrick ever said anything? I mean, has he ever made a sound?"

Marjory thought for a minute. "You mean has he ever said *baaaaa*. No. I'm sure he hasn't. That's strange, isn't it?"

"Unusual, anyway. I think lambs usually bleat all the time," said Russell. "I guess it's because he's never heard a sheep make a sound."

"How would Patrick know anything about sheep?" asked Rosalind. "He's lived with the Millers all his life and the only mother he knows is a dog."

They all looked at Patrick, a fine-looking lamb, sturdy and grayish-white with a black nose and one fluffy white patch of wool on his shoulder.

"Of course," said Marjory slowly. "Patrick doesn't know he's a sheep." Now they all looked at Berta. "He thinks he's a dog."

"Not only a dog, but a dachshund," said Rosalind. She burst out laughing.

"Well, I'm not sure how much lambs think," said Russell. "But he sure doesn't know much about being a sheep."

Marjory patted Berta. "You've done a good job," she said quietly. "But I think it's our turn to teach Patrick something now."

Berta laid her chin on Marjory's knee and sighed. As for Patrick, he stood happily on the grass and waited to learn how to be a sheep.

Marjory, Rosalind and Russell sat and thought. Berta lay with her chin on Marjory's knee, watching Patrick intently. Patrick began to walk around, exploring this new part of his world.

"How will Patrick learn to be a sheep?" Rosalind wondered.

"What does he really need to know?" asked Russell. "I mean, what do sheep do that Patrick absolutely must learn?"

"Eat grass," said Marjory. "He's supposed to live in our yard and eat grass.

Anyway, he can't go on drinking out of a bottle all his life and he can't eat dog food."

"You're right," said Russell. "A sheep has to eat like a sheep. Whether he sounds like a sheep is not so important."

"I don't suppose he'll start barking," said Rosalind, and she laughed again.

"Or acting like a dog," said Marjory. "Maybe that was the problem with Mary's little lamb. You know, in the song. Maybe he followed her to school because he thought he was a dog." She imagined Patrick trotting along after her to school, refusing to go home. He would follow her right up the stairs and into the classroom.

The song was very realistic, she decided. The children would certainly laugh and Mrs. Kent might laugh a little but then she would say, "You're going to have to take that lamb home, Marjory. He can't stay at school, you know."

How embarrassing. But she would always make sure Patrick was fastened by a long cord to the clothesline post. And he would be eating grass. He wouldn't want to come to school.

"We have to teach him to eat grass," she said firmly. "He can learn everything else about being a sheep on his own."

They all thought some more. How could you teach a lamb to eat grass?

"I refuse to eat grass myself," Russell announced, and both girls nodded. They didn't want to eat grass either.

"Patrick is still almost a baby, isn't he?" Rosalind asked.

"I guess so," said Marjory.

"Well, when my little sister was a baby, we chopped up regular food and just put it in her mouth. It was pretty messy but she learned to chew it up and now she eats everything we do."

"I'll get some scissors," said Marjory.

They used the scissors to chop some nice green grass into very small pieces. Marjory took a pinch in her fingers and stuck it into Patrick's mouth. Patrick looked a bit surprised and sucked hard on her fingers, but he didn't spit out the grass.

"He must have swallowed it," said Russell. "Let me try."

They took turns feeding Patrick pinches of grass. Berta watched from the steps, her eyes following every move.

Finally Rosalind said she had to go home. "I think he's learning something," she said hopefully. Her fingers were a little red and sore from being sucked.

"At least he seems to like the taste of grass," said Russell. "I'm positive he'll want more tomorrow."

Marjory led Patrick back onto the porch. Berta got up from her spot on the steps and nudged him toward the box. When he was safely inside and lying down, she jumped in and sniffed him all over. Then she went to sleep.

The next day Patrick ate chopped-up grass from their hands. He nibbled it up with his lips and chewed and swallowed. Berta watched closely from the steps.

The day after that they moved on to what Rosalind called Lesson Three: Eating Grass from the Ground. Russell put a pile of chopped-up grass on top of the growing grass. At first Patrick ignored it, but Marjory pushed his head down until his nose was touching the pile. Then he shook his tail and started to eat. He ate the whole pile of grass. Then he looked hopefully around as if he was waiting for more to fall from the sky.

"He's not brilliant," said Rosalind, "but I bet he'll catch on tomorrow."

"Are sheep ever brilliant?" said Marjory. "Anyway, he's not a sheep yet. He's just a baby. I think he's doing very well. Right, Berta?" But Berta was sound asleep.

The next day it was Marjory's turn to chop the grass and pile it up for Patrick on the lawn. A smaller pile today. That was Lesson Four in their plan. She wasn't going to give Patrick any help, either. She went and joined the others on the steps, with Berta right beside her as usual.

Patrick made short work of the little heap of grass. He seemed puzzled as he snuffled up the last bits, and he looked at Marjory for a moment. Then he lowered his head and took another bite. This time he was eating the grass that was growing. The children were so quiet that they could hear the grass stems snapping between his teeth.

Patrick lifted his head. Marjory could

see blades of grass sticking out of his mouth. He began to chew. In a moment he had chewed up and swallowed that whole mouthful of grass.

He stood there a moment almost as if he was thinking. Then he opened his mouth and said *baaaaa* quite loudly. He looked a little surprised and then he said it again. *Baaaaaaa*. Then he bent his head and began to eat grass steadily.

Berta lifted her head when Patrick spoke. She didn't move for a moment. Then she sighed a big sigh and stood up.

"It's all right, Berta," said Marjory. "He's just growing up."

But Berta paid no attention. She turned around and crossed the porch toward the house without looking back. She pushed the screen door open with her nose and went inside. They could hear her walk across the living room and up the stairs.

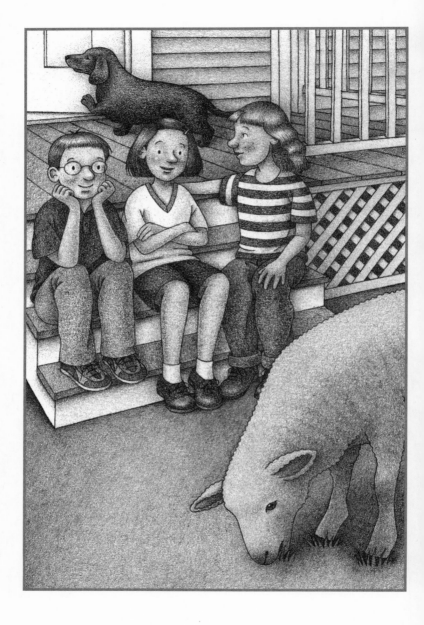

"I guess she thinks Patrick doesn't need her so much now," said Russell. "He's eating grass and he can do that on his own."

"Her job is finished," said Rosalind. "You know Berta isn't the sort to do work that isn't needed."

"I think she knows he's a sheep now. He's not her baby any more," said Marjory. "He told her that when he said *baaaa*. I wonder whether she'll remember that he used to be her baby."

They all sat thinking about that and watching Patrick eat. Just about the time he had finally had enough, Mr. Miller came home.

After Marjory and Rosalind and Russell told him everything that had happened, he said, "You've taught Patrick what he needs to know. He's ready to become a regular farm animal. You and Berta have done a fine job."

"But what will happen to Patrick now?" asked Marjory.

"He'll sleep in the barn. I've got a nice pen all ready for him. And he'll be able to eat grass all day. He will be a very happy sheep."

Marjory knew he was right, but she also knew that she would miss Patrick the lamb. Patrick the sheep wouldn't be quite the same.

When Rosalind and Russell had gone home, she went to find Berta. It wasn't hard since she was back in her old forbidden spot on Marjory's bed. Asleep.

Marjory looked at her sleeping dog. Did she think she had done a fine job? Would she miss Patrick? Would she visit him while he ate grass?"

"Oh, I wish you could talk," she said. She lay down on the bed. Berta moved over a tiny bit to make room for her.

"You're a funny dog," said Marjory. "I don't understand you but it's nice to have you back where you're not supposed to be."

CHAPTER 10
BERTA'S BABIES

Patrick spent the whole summer eating grass in the Millers' yard. He did such a good job of keeping it trimmed that no one ever had to mow. He grew and grew and his wool was thick. The white patch on his shoulder gradually disappeared, and he was medium gray from head to tail.

He also said *baaaaaa* over and over, all day long.

"Maybe he's waiting for another sheep to answer him," said Russell.

"Or maybe he just likes the sound of his own voice," said Rosalind.

"I love Patrick but I'm tired of the sound of his voice," said Marjory. "I tell him to be quiet, but sheep don't seem to listen very well."

Berta paid no attention to Patrick's voice. In fact, she ignored him completely. She had gone back to her old life of eating, sleeping and short walks.

"Doesn't she miss Patrick at all?" Marjory asked her mother. "She loved him so much."

"She was a very good mother," said Mrs. Miller. "She did the job. But animals don't go on being mothers to their children when their children don't need them any more. And the children forget their mothers. Not like people. We never forget."

It was nice having Berta back at her regular job of wagging her tail when Marjory came home from school and keeping her company while she did her homework. Marjory had to admit that.

"You were a terrific mother," she said to Berta. "But what I like best about you is that you are a dog and a good one, too."

In September Patrick went back to the farm where he would have lots of sheep to talk to. Jack Steiner was very pleased with him and his wool when he came to pick him up.

"I told you he was a good one," he said. "And you folks took real good care of him."

"We had help," said Mr. Miller, looking at Berta. The farmer seemed a little puzzled, but he was in a hurry so he didn't ask questions.

In October Berta had puppies, real dachshund puppies. Mrs. Miller had found a nice dog from a nearby town to be their father, but as far as Berta was concerned, they were her puppies and no one else's.

There were four of them and they were brown just like Berta, but their eyes were closed and their noses were pushed in so that their faces were wrinkly. Their ears were little fat pads that stuck out from the sides of their heads. Mrs. Miller said that they would grow up to look exactly like Berta, but Marjory thought they were darling just the way they were.

Berta became a total mother again. She took charge of the puppies just as she had taken charge of Patrick. And these babies were perfect for her. She could feed them herself. They lined up along her belly sucking away. When they were finished, she could wash them completely, turning them over with her nose and licking them until she decided they were clean. She could curl up around them and keep them cozy in

their box in the kitchen. And everyone, Rosalind included, knew that Berta would protect her babies from any harm.

"Do you think she's so good because she practiced on Patrick?" asked Marjory.

"Practice helps," said her mother. "But I think Berta is just good at being a mother, no matter what sort of babies she has. She knows what to do."

The puppies grew, of course. When their eyes were open and they were beginning to push themselves up on their feet and wobble around their box, Berta sometimes disappeared. The puppies would be squeaking with hunger and Berta nowhere in sight.

Marjory would go upstairs and look under her bed. In the farthest corner she could see a familiar dark shape.

"Berta, come out," she would say sternly. "Your babies are hungry."

Gradually, Berta would creep out and go slowly downstairs to do her job.

"Do you think Berta is bored with her babies?" Marjory asked her father.

"No," he answered. "Every parent needs a break sometimes. And she knows they're big enough to do without her for a while."

Marjory remembered Berta and Patrick curled up together. She remembered how determined Berta was to take over the job of raising Patrick. And she remembered what a big and wonderful baby Patrick turned out to be. She wondered if Berta was just a tiny bit disappointed in her puppies. After all, they would never be sheep.

She mentioned this to Rosalind one day.

"Berta chose Patrick to be her baby," Marjory said. "Maybe she wishes that all her babies would be so special."

"Well," said Rosalind, "don't tell her I said so, but I think that Berta is the one who is special. And I think that any baby of hers will be special, too. In fact, my mother said I could have one of her puppies. Do you think Berta would mind?"

"I'm sure she wouldn't," said Marjory. "In fact, once the puppy grows up and lives at your house, she won't even remember it. Berta likes her babies and then she likes to rest and forget about them. But we'll remember. Imagine, two remarkable dogs right next door to each other. It will be perfect."

Ticket to Curlew
Celia Barker Lottridge

WINNER
Canadian Library Association Book of the Year Award
Geoffrey Bilson Historical Fiction Award

It is 1915, and Sam Ferrier and his father arrive by train in Curlew, Alberta, to build a new home for the family. When they finally reach their parcel of land, Sam can see nothing but endless stretches of grassland and blue sky. It is nothing like their old home in Iowa, and he wonders why his restless father ever decided to bring the family to this lonely, barren land.

In time, though, the house is built, and the rest of the family joins them. Gradually Sam discovers that there is much more to the flat and featureless prairie than he realized. The tall grasses hide a mysterious collection of gleaming white skulls. Torrential thunderstorms appear with startling swiftness out of a clear-blue sky. And when one day he finds that his little brother has suddenly disappeared on the seemingly flat prairie, Sam discovers that their new land can be both awesome and frightening.

ISBN 0-88899-221-1 (paperback)

Wings to Fly
Celia Barker Lottridge

WINNER
IODE National Chapter: Violet Downey Book Award

In *Ticket to Curlew*, Sam Ferrier and his father moved to Canada and built a homestead in the middle of the unsettled prairie. Eventually the rest of the family joined them, and during the first three years they learned to respect their harsh new land and find hidden beauty in its endless grassland.

Eleven-year-old Josie is well settled in her new home now, but she's never had a friend her own age. So when a girl named Margaret moves to the area from England, Josie is glad to have someone with whom she can ride to school, explore the mysterious, abandoned silver house and dream about the future.

But what does the future hold for a young girl in 1918? Could Josie fly airplanes like Katherine Stinson, her heroine?

Will she be a teacher like Miss Barnett? What would it be like to be Margaret's sad mother, who can't bear to unpack her fine English china in the crude sod house that is her new prairie home?

As the year unfolds, Josie searches for more information about the woman aviator. She finds a way to break through Margaret's mother's sadness. And she finally discovers the secret behind the silver house.

ISBN 0-88899-346-3 (paperback)

The Wind Wagon
Celia Barker Lottridge
illustrated by Daniel Clifford

In 1859 the only way to get out west to the Rocky Mountains is by oxcart — and that's a slow journey that takes several months. So when Sam Peppard builds his "wind wagon" — a narrow wooden cart with a large mast in the middle — and announces that he's going to sail across the prairie, everyone scoffs. But Sam sticks to his plan and dreams of mining silver in the Rocky Mountains while waiting for the right wind. And one day, when the wind is almost perfect, he "sets sail" for the West.

Based on a real-life event, this is an exciting and fast-paced story.

ISBN 0-88899-234-3 (paperback)

LOCATING
TROPHY WHITETAILS

DAVID MORRIS

NORTH AMERICAN HUNTING CLUB

Minneapolis, Minnesota

NORTH AMERICAN HUNTING CLUB

Mike Vail	Vice President, Products and Business Development
Tom Carpenter	Director of Book and New Media Development
Steve Perlstein	Book Products Development Manager
Dan Kennedy	Book Development Coordinator
Michele Teigen	Book Development Assistant

This book was originally published by Derrydale Press, Inc.

ISBN 0-914697-93-5

Printed in the United States of America
This book was printed on acid-free paper with 10 percent post-consumer recycled content.

DEDICATION

Dedicated to the thousands of NAHC members who diligently keep our hunting heritage alive and work for wildlife conservation so future generations can enjoy our natural resources.

TABLE OF CONTENTS

EDITOR'S FOREWORD..1

CHAPTER 1
Trophies are Special...5

CHAPTER 2
Basic Ingredients for Trophy Bucks.................15

CHAPTER 3
Sizing up the Trophy Prospects where You Hunt 29

CHAPTER 4
Trophy Prospects across North America.........................43

CHAPTER 5
Region-By-Region Trophy Prospects 53

CHAPTER 6
The Big Picture 75

CHAPTER 7
The Pre-Rut Period 83

CHAPTER 8
The Scraping Period of the Rut 99

CHAPTER 9
The Breeding Period of the Rut.....................115

CHAPTER 10
The Post-Rut Period..129

CHAPTER 11
Closing Thoughts 143

INDEX...147

FOREWORD

When most of us think of white-tailed deer hunting, our minds skip ahead to the moment of truth. In your day dreams a monster buck eases from the brush just where you'd expect him to. He stops with head held high, testing the vagaries of the wind with flared nostrils. The front half of his body is in the clear so you carefully steady the crosshairs or rest the tip of your sight pin right in the crease behind his shoulder and....

Making such a daydream become a reality is where the bullet meets the lands! For each second of such fantasy become reality there are hours, days and weeks of preparation and planning. A huge part of that preparation is finding the place, the precise spot where you can put yourself and that monster buck on a collision course for destiny.

Giving you the knowledge and woods lore to make that happen is what Locating Trophy Whitetails is all about. The author shares his hard-won knowledge of how to find the right spot to take your next trophy buck...and the next...and the next!

From scouting with note pad, topo maps and telephone to wearing out the boot leather in his off-season scouting, David Morris has done it season after season through decades of whitetail hunting. Along the way he has found a few shortcuts which will prove priceless to hunters who canít devote the hours he does to haunting the haunts of trophy bucks.

North American Hunting Club members are white-tailed deer hunters! This book will help put everyone of us in the right place at the right time to make our dreams come true! Enjoy!

Sincerely,

Bill Miller
Executive Director

CHAPTER ONE

TROPHIES ARE SPECIAL

The thought, "What manner of animal is this?" probably first formed in my mind on a cold, windy afternoon in Georgia during the very early years of my hunting career. I already had several small and a couple of medium-sized bucks to my credit, but a really big buck still eluded me. I was in the process of helping my wife into a treestand high on a hill overlooking a recently harvested soybean field when I cast a casual glance toward another large bean field several hundred yards to my left. Much to my surprise, a whopper buck was nervously trotting down a narrow hedgerow winding through the middle of the field.

Excitement got the best of me, and I foolishly launched a couple of absurdly long "hail mary" shots into the teeth of a 30-mile-per-hour crosswind. Due to the wind and the distance, the buck had no idea where the shots came from and I had no idea where they went. Uncertain of where the danger lay, the buck ducked into the thin cover of the hedgerow and miraculously disappeared. Rifle ready, I waited for several minutes for the buck to show himself in the skimpy hedgerow, but nothing not pushed by the wind moved.

Turning to my wife, I shouted above the wind, "He laid down in the hedgerow. I'm going after him. Stay here and watch for him. Signal me if you see him."

With that, I departed posthaste for the hedgerow, checking back occasionally for a sign from my wife but receiving nothing more than a shoulder shrug. When I reached the hedgerow, I began my slow stalk, rifle at port arms. I entered the hedgerow well above where the buck had disappeared, assured by my wife that he was still somewhere in that thin ribbon of brush. As I eased along, I began to doubt that a 200-plus-pound buck with sizable display of bone on his head could possibly hide in the scant cover afforded by the carpet of honeysuckle vines and the scattered persimmon and honey locust trees that made up this hedgerow. The farther I went, the more skeptical I became, despite my wife's assurance that the buck had not left that hedgerow.

Upon reaching the point where the buck had vanished, a shallow, honeysuckle-choked drainage ditch began to run through the center of the hedgerow, forcing me to proceed along the edge rather than the center. Looking ahead, I could see that the hedgerow wound another 100 yards before petering out, leaving only the broomsedge and honeysuckle-rimmed ditch to make its way to the thick pines some 75 yards farther on. If the buck was still around, and all evidence said he was, he had to be between me and the end of the hedgerow.

I proceeded on red alert but not without considerable skepticism. Yard after yard, nothing, not even an obvious place for a buck to hide. Frequent checks with my wife assured me the buck had not slipped out, at least via any visible route. I continued down the left side of the hedgerow until only 15 yards remained. Still no sign of the buck. I had all but given up when the ground in front of me erupted into a huge buck. No time to marvel over where he had come from. Time to act!

The big buck immediately put the hedgerow between him and me, and I immediately set sail to remedy that.

Brimming with anticipation, I knew I had him. With me right on his tail, there was no way the buck could cross that wide open 75 yards to the woods without me getting off two or three good shots.

I burst forth from the hedgerow, head snapping left and right, ready to shoot ... but the buck was nowhere to be seen. Frantic, I ran forward 10 yards for a better view. The soybean field remained empty. Desperate, I turned to my wife on the far hill for help. Upon seeing me look her way, she held both arms straight in front of her and began pointing frantically toward the ground. Precious seconds passing, my mind raced. *The ground? He went to the ground?* Then, it hit me. *The ditch!*

Even as I raced toward the ditch, my eyes futilely traced its course to the woods. Refusing to believe the buck had gotten away so completely unscathed, I half expected to find him burrowed up somewhere in the three-foot-deep crevice as I ran alongside it for several yards. But alas, the tracks told the story, almost as clearly as my wife did later on!

The buck had indeed escaped down the ditch. Deep, splayed running tracks marred the full length of the silty ditch bottom. His escape was so slick and completely un-detected, at least by me, that I first believed he must have belly crawled that 75 yards, but his far-apart tracks told me that wasn't so, as did my wife who had observed it all through binoculars from her elevated vantage point. Hug-ging the ground, he had run flat out down that ditch, his well-adorned head held low and outstretched. He had pulled off an impossible escape and denied me his pres-ence on my wall when I had him cold! As I stood there and looked at those tracks, the thought first hit me, "What manner of animal is this?"

I've spent some 25 years trying to figure out the answer

to that question with only partial success. What I have concluded with absolute certainty, however, is that trophy bucks are different and very special. They are so different, in fact, from lesser bucks and does that they might as well be an entirely separate species. And unless a hunter recognizes that and hunts them accordingly, he simply will not take trophy bucks with any consistency. With that in mind, two questions arise. One, what is a trophy whitetail? Two, how are they different? Let's try to answer those questions.

The term "trophy whitetail" can be defined on two different levels. The first is the personal level, which is based on pride of accomplishment and may have absolutely nothing to do with size. No one can dispute it if a hunter considers a buck he shot to be a "prized memento of one's personal accomplishment," as one dictionary defines "trophy." Under this definition, what constitutes a trophy varies with each hunter and is dependent on where he hunts, his hunting experience, the time available to hunt and the hunting conditions. That's why a yearling four-pointer can rightfully be considered a "trophy" by a beginner tagging his first buck.

For our purposes, however, a definition based on pride of accomplishment rather than size is much too subjective and variable. We need a more objective, size-related definition, yet one that does take into account the very real size difference in bucks from various regions across the continent. Certainly, the words "trophy buck" conjure up an image of a mature, big-racked buck in the minds of most hunters. From this collective perspective, we can define a trophy whitetail as a mature buck, at least 3½ years old, with antlers large enough to rank him among the best bucks consistently taken in a given area.

Why choose 3½ years as the minimum age for a mature buck? While it's true that bucks normally reach their

A mature whitetail buck is almost like a different species from younger bucks and does. His armor is almost complete, and hunting him is one of the greatest challenges in the hunting world.

greatest size between the ages of 5½ and 7½, only a small percentage of the bucks in North America survive to reach this age. Bucks 5½ years old and older are practically non-existent in most deer populations, so to evaluate trophy prospects based around bucks of this age would eliminate most populations from consideration. On the other hand, bucks younger than 3½ simply don't have the antler size or the survival savvy to be called "mature" or to be given the lofty label of "trophy" by serious hunters. But, a 3½-year-old can have impressive antlers and, especially when pressured, can exhibit the uncanny survival skills unique to the trophy whitetail buck.

Now, as for how trophy bucks differ and why they're so special, you need to start with the animal itself. Whitetails as a species are among the most intelligent and adaptable of all animals. What other big game animal can live, yeah even prosper, right under the nose of man? These smart, adaptable creatures have now had a couple of hundred years of intense pressure to hone to a fine edge their survival instincts, and that's the case with just your average, run-of-the-mill whitetail. Now, let's go to the smartest of the smart—trophy bucks. By nature, old, big-racked bucks are the most reclusive members of the clan, and if that weren't enough, they've been made even more reclusive by being the most sought-after of their species. It's literally a matter of get smart or get dead for trophy bucks, and they've answered the call quite admirably. So admirably, in fact, that, except during the rut, they have very little in common with does or lesser bucks, either in their behavior or where they live, and are largely nocturnal, or will become that way at the first sign of pressure. To fully understand these remarkable animals, you need to understand the aging process and the changes they go through.

For 20 years, I managed the 13,000-acre Burnt Pine Plantation in middle Georgia. Our guests harvested close to 1,500 bucks during that time. The plantation was a great place to study and observe deer. And study them we did. Our biologists kept meticulous records of the deer sighted and harvested by guests. In addition, they conducted off-season deer censuses and, among other things, classified all bucks seen into one of three age groups—1½-, 2½- and 3½-year-old or older. Over the years, we collected vast amounts of consistent data that gave us a very accurate idea of our deer density, buck/doe ratio and, very importantly, our buck age structure. From all this, we were to draw certain conclusions about the vulnerability of each buck age class by comparing the ages of the bucks sighted or killed by hunters with the known buck age structure of the population. Those conclusions clearly showed the fast accelerating difficulty of killing a buck with each passing year.

A 1½-year-old buck is a pretty easy target. He's naive, eager and often too bold for his own good, about like a teenage boy out on his own for the first time and just discovering girls. He's driven by the rutting urge but is not sure what to do about it. Yearling bucks have little compunction about moving during daylight hours and frequent major feeding areas or any other place the crowd hangs out. Just hunt deer and you'll find 1½-year-old bucks. They differ little in vulnerability from does, except they are more naive once you've made contact with them. Without question, the great majority of the bucks killed across the country are yearlings.

Substantial progress is made in a buck's education between 1½ and 2½, but it is only a pale foreshadowing of what is to come. The naive, almost air-headed attitude of his first year has now given way to a measured caution and the realization, just a mild suspicion, that danger may be near at any time.

The 2½-year-old is strongly attracted by the lure of the rut and will demonstrate obvious confidence in the presence of does, fawns and yearlings. They tend to spend considerable time around doe groups and major food sources. They will move readily during daylight hours, but not so freely as a year earlier. Hunters after "just bucks" will bump into their share of 2½s, but they are warier and less likely to expose themselves to a hunter's bullet than a yearling. In fact, plantation records say that a 2½-year-old in a hunted population is twice as hard to kill as that same buck at 1½ years old . . . and he's only just started to wise up!

At 3½, a buck has pretty well caught onto the basics of survival but still has room to work on the fine points. With two seasons as a legal target behind and the added maturity time and experience bring, he has learned the dangers and how to avoid them. His travels are deliberate and usually in thicker cover or under the concealment of darkness. He spends less time around the doe groups and more time in his own now well-established core area. Still, he is vulnerable, mainly when his new-found caution is compromised by the rut, but a 3½-year-old buck is far from easy, especially in heavily hunted populations. That fact is driven home by plantation records that argue a buck is three times harder to kill at 3½ than at 2½ and six times harder to kill at 3½ than at 1½! Factor in how few bucks in most areas ever reach the ripe old age of 3½ and you realize why killing a mature buck of any size is quite an accomplishment.

If a buck makes it to 4½, the odds are slim that he'll fall to a hunter's bullet. A buck this age and older is now in the advanced program of whitetail studies. His every move and intent are governed by the drive to survive. He has few weaknesses the hunter can exploit, and about the only time his guard is dropped even briefly is when the scent of a hot doe hangs heavily in the air. Outside the rut, these hunter-wise old bucks are darned near unkillable, especially if pressured, in which case they will become almost totally nocturnal. If they move during daylight hours, it's a safe bet they'll be in thick cover.

Bucks that see the other side of 4½ have the hunters patterned far better than they him. Normal tactics and longtime permanent stands don't pose much of a threat to them. They avoid the doe hangouts and the places frequented by other deer. They are extremely difficult to catch in the open, even on major food sources. Over the years on the plantation, bucks 4½ years old and older were so hard to come by that we couldn't even calculate meaningful odds of killing them! And, it only gets worse with each passing year beyond 4½!

One on one, the trophy whitetail is unquestionably one of the most challenging animals in the world to hunt. Think about it, they live in thick cover; they are all but nocturnal; they are equipped with senses humans cannot hope to match, especially hearing and smell; they are constantly wired and ready to jump out of their skin at the slightest provocation; and on top of all of that, their intelligence seems sufficient for them to teach school at the junior college level if only they could talk. They are just plain tough to line up in a set of rifle sights. Anything more difficult would have to get its edge from remoteness, difficult terrain, harsh climate, scarcity, aggressiveness, or a truly nocturnal nature. The fact is that without the rut to weaken their defenses, the animal-righters would probably have the trophy whitetail listed as "rare and endangered" . . . and we hunters would agree with them!

CHAPTER TWO

BASIC INGREDIENTS FOR TROPHY BUCKS

Many years ago during my early tenure as a bass guide on Georgia's Lake Eufaula, I learned a lesson I've never forgotten. At the time, Eufaula was about the hottest big bass lake going. Six and seven-pounders were commonplace, and eight-pounders hardly turned a regular's head. It took a nine-pound-plus fish to rate trophy status among the lake's hardcore.

On this particular occasion, a couple of chaps from Arkansas had booked me for three days. When I met them at the marina late on the afternoon prior to our trip, I began to probe into their fishing prowess as soon as the niceties were dispensed with.

The first guy was in his late 30s and had the weather-worn look of a man who had spent many an hour under the hot sun having his hide tanned to leather. When I asked him if he fished much, he smiled confidently and said, "About 300 days a year. I'm a full-time guide on Lake Ouachita."

The thought raced through my mind that I had to quit this line of work before my hide became as corrugated as his.

"What about you?" I inquired of his companion.

"Every weekend and holiday, and any other time I can get away from the plant," the athletic-looking 30-year-old said.

Now came the big question—the one I always asked to really size up a guy's fishing ability. In my mind, everything else I might learn about them was secondary. Now I'd find out what kind of fishermen they really were.

"What's your biggest bass?" I asked with a certain note of finality.

"Seven pounds, 14 ounces," came the guide's response.

"Just under 7½," the younger man said proudly.

"Good fish," I responded patronizingly, having now placed them solidly in the "fair fishermen" category based upon their answers.

Well, over the next three days, those "fair fishermen" took me to school on bass fishing. They fished circles around me. When the smoke cleared, they had both topped their previous personal record three or four times and had run up an enviable score on six and seven-pound bass.

As they were preparing to return to Arkansas, one of them occasioned to say, "Great trip and a great lake! You can't catch fish like this at home. They just aren't there."

In that simple statement lies a profound truth I've never forgotten. Nobody, no matter how good he is, can catch, or kill something that isn't there! It's not a question of skill, knowledge, or tactics. Those things only become factors in success when what you seek is present. And, this truth applies just as well to trophy whitetails as to trophy bass.

Countless would-be trophy whitetail hunters go through the motions of hunting trophy bucks year after year and never shoot one for the very same reason those Arkansas fishermen had never caught any really big bass. They are hunting something that is not there—or that exists in such low numbers as to make their chances of success practically nil. The only absolute prerequisite for killing a trophy whitetail is being where there are trophy whitetails! True, to take trophy bucks with any consistency, a hunter *needs*

This great buck, a record-class 10-pointer from South Texas, is a trophy by any standards—but "trophy" doesn't have to apply only to a monster like this.

to have a high level of skill and knowledge, but he *must* hunt where such animals live in appreciable numbers!

Before proceeding, we need to distinguish between the terms "mature" and "trophy." For our purposes, we'll define "mature" as any buck 3½ years old and older. We'll define "trophy" as a *mature* buck big enough to rank among the better bucks consistently taken in an area. This definition requires that a trophy buck be at least 3½ years old and large relative only to the other bucks in that particular area; not necessarily large in absolute terms or in comparison to the bucks in a different location. Thus, our definition works anywhere and takes into account the inherent size differences from one area to another. Much of this discussion will focus on mature bucks since trophy bucks will be a natural by-product of a population of mature bucks.

Every trophy hunter must decide for himself what size buck is big enough to meet his personal trophy standards. Once this is done, he must then realistically evaluate his chances of meeting his standards where he hunts. Or, he can reverse the process—evaluate the trophy prospects where he hunts first and then set his trophy standards based on the largest buck he feels he has a reasonable chance to take there. If the evaluation process leads a hunter to the conclusion that the size he is after is not available where he hunts, he must search elsewhere and be able to calculate his odds there. Anyway you look at it, a trophy hunter needs to be able to size up the trophy prospects where he plans to hunt. There are basically three major considerations in evaluating the trophy prospects of a place. They are the number of mature bucks present, their size, and their huntability. These considerations are influenced by many factors, but no one factor has a greater influence on a given area's overall trophy prospects than hunting pressure. The relationship is simple: the greater the pressure, the poorer the trophy prospects.

THE NUMBER OF MATURE BUCKS PRESENT

The number of mature bucks present is of paramount concern in evaluating trophy prospects. The more mature bucks around, the greater your chances of shooting a trophy. Essentially, three factors contribute to the number of mature bucks. One, the density of the deer population. Two, the buck/doe ratio. And three, the buck age structure. The latter two are largely determined by buck hunting pressure. Let's look at each one.

Herd Density:
All things being equal, greater deer densities should mean more mature bucks and greater odds of trophy success. It's simple arithmetic. For instance, if two tracts of land have similar buck/doe ratios and buck age structures but one tract has twice as many deer as the other, which tract offers you the best chance of seeing a mature buck? The tract with twice as many deer offers you twice the odds!

On the other hand, herd density can be a two-sided coin for the trophy hunter. Too many deer means overpopulation, which reduces antler size due to poor nutrition. For the trophy hunter, the abundance of deer and where the herd stands relative to the carrying capacity of the land are both important concerns.

I generally consider herd density to be the least important of the three factors, but there are a few places where overall deer numbers are so low as to be only marginally huntable. Examples can be seen on the fringe of the whitetail's range in such places as the vast northern forests of Canada and parts of Mexico. Such extremely low populations are the exception, and ample numbers of deer exist just about everywhere whitetails are hunted. The fact is that trophy hunting can be quite good even in relatively low populations. I would much rather hunt an area with few deer and a tight buck/doe ratio and good buck age structure than a high density herd with a disproportionate number of does and a shot-out buck population.

Buck/Doe Ratio:

One of the major ways in which hunting pressure impacts a deer herd is in the ratio of "adult" (1½ years old and older) bucks to adult does, known simply as the buck/doe ratio. Generally speaking, the buck/doe ratio is "higher" or "tighter," meaning more bucks in relation to does, in lightly hunted populations and "lower" or "wider" in heavily hunted herds, especially those with disproportionate pressure on bucks. Fawns are not included in the buck/doe ratio; therefore, the ratio between antlered and antlerless deer will reflect an even greater spread, sometimes nearly twice as much since a healthy herd can average close to a fawn per adult doe in the fall. As a result, a buck/doe ratio of, say, 1:3 could mean an antlered/antlerless ratio of around 1:6. Antlerless sightings could give the wrong impression of the buck/doe ratio without taking this into account.

The buck/doe ratio is simply a means of expressing the makeup of the adult deer herd. It can be easily translated into percentages. For instance, a buck/doe ratio of 1:1 means 50 percent are bucks and 50 percent are does; a 1:2 translates into 33 percent bucks and 67 percent does; a 1:3 ratio results in 25 versus 75 percent; and so on.

With this understanding, it is easy to see that the

buck/doe ratio has a direct bearing on the number of bucks in the population. Assuming a piece of property is capable of carrying only so many deer without sacrificing size, then it is obviously to the trophy hunter's advantage to have as many bucks represented in that population as possible. The lower the buck/doe ratio, the greater the percentage and the higher the total number of bucks present. And, logic dictates that more bucks in a herd leads to a greater likelihood that mature bucks are present. As for does, it is only necessary to have enough to replenish the losses each year, assuming the herd is at carrying capacity. A buck/doe ratio unnecessarily weighted toward does means space is occupied by does that could be filled by bucks.

Buck Age Structure:

Unquestionably, the most damaging impact of hunting pressure on trophy prospects is seen in the buck age structure, which is simply the distribution of bucks throughout the various age classes. High hunting pressure results in fewer mature bucks and lower trophy prospects. Light hunting pressure assures the ample presence of mature bucks, greatly enhancing the trophy outlook. Age is, after all, the most limiting factor in trophy production across the country, and hunting pressure more than anything else will determine how many bucks survive to reach maturity.

Summarizing, the herd density determines the total number of deer present. The buck/doe ratio determines how many of the deer are bucks. The buck age structure determines how many of the bucks are mature, which translates directly into the number of trophies available.

Nutrition, genetics and the ability to survive to maturity are among the key requirements for large antlers. Some areas produce better bucks than others, so "trophy" is a very subjective term.

THE SIZE OF THE MATURE BUCKS

Region-To-Region Size Differences:

Most serious trophy hunters are well aware that great differences exist in the size of bucks, even those of the same age, from region to region across the country. Even under identical and ideal conditions, some places inherently produce relatively small deer; others grow medium-sized deer; and still others turn out large deer. This difference in size is where genetics and nutrition enter the picture . . . and, as taxonomists would say, so do the subspecies differences. For the traveling hunter interested in hunting the biggest bucks available, the inherent difference in size from one place to another is an important consideration in his analysis of trophy prospects.

Factors Affecting Size At A Given Place:

Let's now see how the three cornerstones of buck size—genetics, nutrition and age—figure into the trophy prospects of one particular area. Genetics determine the size potential of the bucks at any given age. The quality of nutrition determines how much of that size potential is actually realized at a given age. Last, but certainly not least in the equation, sufficient age is required for bucks to reach their maximum size under the existing genetic and nutritional realities.

In reality, the full size potential of bucks is seldom achieved. Most often, realization of the size potential is limited by inadequate nutrition, largely from over-crowding, and the lack of age, mainly due to hunting pressure. It is even possible for the natural genetic potential of a herd to be eroded through the heavy, long-term harvest of the better-antlered bucks.

The fact is that most of us can do little to change the

existing genetic, nutritional, and age status of a deer herd. While it is helpful to understand their roles, there is not much point in dwelling on the "potential" of a place (unless you are in a position to manage that place to better achieve full size potential). Rather, most trophy hunters are better served simply by determining the size of the mature bucks actually being taken in a given place, or put another way, how much of the potential is actually being realized.

To that end, there are a couple of aspects of interest. One, the *average* size of the mature bucks. Two, the *range of sizes* represented by the mature bucks within the herd. This second aspect, the size range, is a critical factor in determining the number of better-than-average mature bucks, i.e., trophy bucks, and the realistic top-end size. While nutrition and genetics play critical roles in the size attained by mature bucks at any particular location, the variable most often of foremost concern to trophy hunters is the buck age structure, which, of course, is a function of hunting pressure. Let's take a closer look at how hunting pressure affects both the average size and range of sizes of mature bucks.

In lightly hunted populations, bucks of all ages are present. In heavily pressured herds, relatively few bucks even reach maturity and bucks older than 3½ are downright rare. However, a buck is not as big at 3½ years old as he will be at 5½, 6½, or 7½ years old, normally considered peak antler years. It is easy to see that a population of bucks distributed throughout *all* the "mature" age classes, 3½ to 9½, will *average* older and bigger and will span a *greater range* of sizes than a population whose mature bucks are primarily 3½-year-olds. In a population with a well-distributed buck age structure, the top-end size will be greater because of the increased presence of peak-sized 5½-, 6½- and 7½-year-old bucks. It's simply a matter of more bucks reaching the age necessary to achieve their genetic potential under existing nutritional conditions.

BUCK HUNTABILITY

While trophy bucks must be present before a hunter has any hope of success, the hunter still has to be able to kill them. Even when the numbers are the same, the degree of difficulty in hunting trophy bucks, that is, their "huntability", varies from place to place. Buck huntability is a definite factor in sizing up the trophy prospects of a place, but it ranks well behind mature buck numbers and size in importance.

Many factors bear on buck huntability. For instance, timing of the season is a big one. If the hunting season fails to coincide with the rut, buck huntability is greatly reduced. Another factor is the herd density relative to the carrying capacity. In overcrowded herds, deer will concentrate on food sources and tend to move more during daylight hours because they have to feed longer and more often since quality food is in short supply. Access to hunting land and certainly the size of the properties that can be hunted by an individual also figure into huntability. Obviously, weather, moon phases and the like enter the picture, but these things have a temporary impact and that impact is essentially the same from place to place. There are, however, two overriding variables affecting buck huntability that we'll focus on here. They are hunting pressure (there it is again) and habitat conditions.

Hunting pressure both suppresses and alters deer activity. The more pressure, the less daylight movement and the less predictability in deer patterns. Even rutting activity is suppressed by high pressure. Feeding patterns are affected to an even greater degree. The extent to which deer react to human pressure should not be underestimated. Normal movement patterns are easily disrupted, and the deer can become virtually nocturnal, especially trophy bucks.

Since the rut is such a critical part of trophy hunting, a closer look at how hunting pressure affects buck huntability during the rut is helpful. Besides the simple harassment factor, which in itself forces the deer to alter their patterns, hunting pressure brings structural and behavioral changes to the deer herd that are detrimental to rutting activity.

First, heavy pressure adversely impacts the buck age structure by reducing both the percentage and the actual number of mature bucks in a herd. Beyond the obvious harm done by reduced numbers, this results in a buck population made up largely of immature bucks that have not yet developed the competitiveness or the rutting behavioral patterns (we'll discuss these later) characteristic of mature bucks. As a result, traditional rutting patterns and activities break down and the rut is fragmented, non-competitive and indistinct. Even the few mature bucks in such a population fail to establish clear rutting patterns since the natural structure of the herd has broken down. Next, heavy pressure results in a wider buck/doe ratio, which further results in an indistinct, spread-out rut. The ready availability of does reduces the competition between bucks. Most of the breeding and rutting activity takes place at night. Daylight movement is spotty and unpredictable. Rutting sign is halfhearted and undependable. All in all, this situation makes for very tough trophy hunting.

By contrast, a tighter buck/doe ratio is accompanied by a

more competitive rut. More of the ritual activities associated with the rut, which are of greater importance to the trophy hunter than the breeding *per se*, are played out in daylight hours as the bucks vie for dominance and the relatively limited supply of does. Bucks lay down more sign, and this sign can be hunted with some predictability. Bucks spend more time during this period preoccupied with the rut rather than survival. That spells opportunity for the trophy hunter.

HABITAT AND HUNTABILITY:

The huntability of the habitat is a key consideration independent of hunting pressure. Here, we're talking about how the characteristics of the country affect the huntability of bucks. There are some places that are just plain hard to hunt. Thick cover, rough terrain, swampy conditions, inaccessibility, large, unbroken tracts of uniform cover etc., can reduce your odds even though the trophy bucks are there. Still, I much prefer tough hunting country with trophy bucks than easy country without them!

In summary, the most skilled whitetail hunter in the world using the most deadly tactics ever devised will not kill a trophy whitetail where none exist. That being the case, the first thing a trophy hunter must do is accurately size up the trophy prospects where he hunts. Are trophy bucks present in huntable numbers? What size trophy is a realistic possibility? What are the real odds of success? Without the answers to these questions, you may be hunting something that simply is not there!

CHAPTER THREE

SIZING UP THE TROPHY PROSPECTS WHERE YOU HUNT

Height scares me, especially when I'm on a tiny platform so high that a prowling hawk can fly by 25 feet *below* my stand! That's just the predicament I found myself in that chilly November morning in middle Georgia. While still-hunting the afternoon before, I had found a series of scrapes and rubs along a stream bordering a large clearcut. The sign was that of a mature buck, and in all likelihood, he spent much of his time in the head-high tangle of briars, honeysuckle and pines in the four-year-old cutover. The cover was too thick to hunt from the ground, but the high hill at the top edge of the clearcut seemed to offer a good vantage point.

Even as I hung the treestand that night in the dim glow of the headlights of my Suburban, I had the sensation of excessive height. Yet it wasn't until dawn broke the next morning that I realized what I had done. Not only was my stand too high for my liking, probably 20 feet above the ground, but the tree I had selected was on the edge of a precipitous drop-off. For better or worse, there I was, a safety belt my only life insurance. But the thought of dangling by the waist 20 feet above the ground didn't exactly calm my jittery nerves.

As my thoughts returned to the task at hand, my stare shifted from the scrapeline some 200 yards away just long enough to cast a glance toward the staggered row of tree steps that invited me to escape while the escaping was good. Rejecting the invitation, my eyes returned to the scrapes...and to the buck working them. He had seemingly materialized from nowhere.

"How do they do that?" I wondered as I secured my grip on the tree with one hand and raised my binoculars with the other.

"An eight-pointer," I registered, the judging process beginning automatically. "Good main beams. Above average mass. Fair width, maybe 18 inches. Strong brows, good G-2s and fair G-3s. He'll top 130. I'm taking him."

After no small amount of squirming and fidgeting, I finally maneuvered into a position that seemed both steady and secure. I barely heard the shot or felt the recoil of the .280 Remington, but I did hear the telltale "whomp" of the 140-grain Nosler striking home. There was no need to get in a hurry exiting that tree and regaining a grip on life more secure than the width of a safety-belt strap.

Late November is cold in northwest Montana. Despite the three-mile walk to my hunting area, I was still plenty chilly. Fine ice crystals were falling from clear skies as I set up to rattle. Big, dragging tracks through the six inches of snow and two doormat-sized scrapes pawed out to bare ground had made me decide on this spot. I slid under the overhanging limbs of a spruce tree located at the intersection of two abandoned logging roads. A slight breeze wafted into the thick stand of lodgepole pines in front of me. Dense larch provided good cover behind. After the prerequisite limb rubbing, I began rattling, tickling the antlers together to start with and gradually gaining volume and intensity.

Trophy size varies by region. In Georgia, where the author shot this 4½-year old 130-class buck, such a deer is a fine trophy, but in areas such as the Midwest and Central Canada such a buck would be well below the average for mature whitetails.

I was no more than 20 seconds into the ruse when I saw hurried movement to my right. A buck was coming . . . fast. At first sight of him, my heart sputtered a time or two then kicked into overdrive. He was wide, maybe 24 inches, and very tall. He pulled up from his swing downwind no more than 10 yards away. I needed no binoculars to see he was an eight-pointer. Exceptional tines pushed his score well into the 140s. His only drawback was a lack of mass. I let him go, which he did with admirable haste.

Encouraged, I hit the antlers again. Within moments, a second buck slipped into the logging road 80 yards downwind. His head snapped around as he got a nostril full of my scent. Expecting a fight and baffled by the inconsistency, he stared hard in my direction. I sized him up through nine-power magnification.

"A solid 10-pointer," my mind recorded. "Long tines. Even G-4s are long, at least seven inches. About 19 wide. He'll score high, probably 150."

To take bucks like this 160-class Saskatchewan 10-pointer, you simply must hunt where such bucks live. Regardless of skill, experience, or determination, you can't find something that isn't there!

My safety slid forward, and the crosshairs steadied on his shoulder. One second, two seconds, three . . . I lowered my rifle even as the buck vanished into the trees. He was good, very good, but I could not bring myself to shoot him with over a week left in the Montana season.

Why would I shoot a 130-class buck in Georgia but pass up a 150-class buck in Montana? Because I knew what the trophy prospects were in both places. I was fully aware that a 130-class buck was about as big as I had a reasonable chance to harvest in Georgia. On the other hand, the area of Montana I was hunting produces 150s with some regularity and a 160 or better is an outside possibility during the peak of rut. Without this knowledge, I could have easily made a mistake . . . like passing up a 130 in Georgia while holding out for a 150 or like shooting a 130 in Montana where a 150 or better is a realistic possibility. The futility of hunting something that isn't there or the lost opportunity represented by shooting a buck well below the trophy standards of the area can be largely prevented by accurately sizing up the trophy prospects where you hunt.

In the previous chapter, we saw that there are three main considerations in evaluating trophy prospects—the number of mature bucks, their size and their huntability—and we probed some of the factors affecting each. With this background, let's now move to practical application.

First, we'll look more closely at hunting pressure—the greatest single factor influencing the relative number (and to a lesser degree, the size) of mature bucks across the continent and a major indicator of the hunting prospects in a place. Second, we'll look at the critical role the actual place-to-place size differences of bucks play in what a trophy hunter can hope to shoot in a given area. Then, we'll see how combining these two factors in graph-form can go a long way toward sizing up the trophy prospects in a given area.

QUANTIFYING THE LEVEL OF PRESSURE

The importance of hunting pressure in trophy hunting cannot be overstated. As we've seen, the higher the pressure, the lower the trophy prospects; or conversely, the lower the pressure, the higher the trophy prospects. So, if a person could somehow quantify the hunting pressure in his area, he would have a good start on sizing up the trophy prospects. While biologists and game managers do have ways of accurately quantifying the effects of hunting pressure based on harvest data and scientific formulas, that kind of tedium is best left to the professionals. Besides, we hunters don't need that kind of detail to find the answers we need.

Fortunately, experience and a common-sense analysis of the hunting situation where you hunt can allow you to categorize the level of hunting pressure accurately enough to tell you a lot about the trophy prospects. To that end, I categorize relative hunting pressure into three levels—light, moderate and heavy. After a quick look at the characteristics of each, you will probably have no trouble recognizing which is most applicable to your area.

A *lightly hunted* area is characterized by a high percentage of mature bucks, including some 5½s, 6½s and 7½s, in the antlered buck population. Less than 25 percent of the antlered bucks are harvested per year. The buck/doe ratio is good, perhaps 1:1.5 or so. Competition between hunters is minimal. Deer move freely during daylight hours on somewhat predictable patterns. A distinct, competitive rut is accompanied by an abundance of buck sign and rutting activity. Today only remote, protected, or thinly populated areas have light hunting pressure, or perhaps areas with very restrictive and/or short seasons.

Areas with *moderate hunting pressure* have a fair number of mature bucks, but most are 3½s and 4½s. Bucks 5½-years-old and older are taken occasionally but are hard to come by. Young bucks make up most of the harvest since from 30 to 65 percent of the antlered bucks are shot each year. Does substantially outnumber antlered bucks, and ratios of 1:2 to 1:4 can be expected, depending on antlerless regulations and the reproductive rate. Hunter competition is clearly evident, but enough solitude is possible for a "quality" experience. Deer movement is somewhat suppressed and altered, and overall daytime activity is largely limited to early morning and late afternoon hours. Mature bucks tend to be primarily nocturnal, especially outside the rut. The rut is fairly well defined but often sporadic. Buck sign is present and huntable, though inconsistent. Moderate pressure is the most prevalent trophy hunting situation in the U.S. today, and the quality of trophy hunting varies considerably depending on where in the moderate pressure range a place falls.

In *heavy pressure* areas, mature bucks are outright rare, as you would expect when 65 to 95 percent of the antlered bucks are shot each year. The few mature bucks that do exist are nearly all 3½s. A 5½ or older is a real novelty. Yearling bucks make up the great majority of the harvest. The buck/doe ratio heavily favors does, and antlered bucks of any size are hard to pass up ... and to find. Hunter competition is keen, and it is not easy for a hunter to distance himself from the presence or evidence of other hunters. Most deer activity is at night or very early or late in the day. Forced movement accounts for much of the harvest. The rut is a sad affair. Rutting activity and sign are spotty and inconsistent. Trophy hunting in heavily pressured areas is a most difficult game and pretty much limited to hunting a known buck or the most inaccessible areas. The more populated areas of the East and South are subjected to heavy pressure.

ILLUSTRATING THE IMPACT OF PRESSURE

The impact of hunting pressure on the number and size of mature bucks can be graphically illustrated. The following graphs will show far better than words how the various levels of pressure affect the trophy prospects in a given herd.

THE IMPACT OF PRESSURE

How various levels of hunting pressure affect the size and number of mature bucks present in any given place.

GROSS B&C SCORE OF MATURE BUCKS

Comparing these curves plainly shows the impact different levels of pressure can have on a herd. First, note the difference in the total number of mature bucks as revealed by the maximum height of the curve. In truth, the actual numerical difference between heavy pressure and light pressure is even greater than our "relative number" curves are depicting. In very heavily hunted areas, the high pressure curve would hardly even be a blip on the graph. Want to guess what your odds of shooting any mature buck would be in such a place?

Next, look on the size line where the curves peak. This represents the average size of mature bucks in a given herd. On the light pressure curve, the average size is 125. On the moderate curve, it's about 115. The heavy pressure curve barely squeaks out 105. Why? Because under heavy pressure, nearly all the mature bucks are 3½. Under moderate, there are more older thus larger bucks. When the pressure is light, there are even more older and larger bucks to pull the average size even higher.

For the serious trophy hunter, the curve's righthand extension beyond the peak is the telling feature. (Remember, our definition of a trophy is a mature buck large enough to be among the best consistently taken in a given area.) This part of the curve defines the true trophy prospects by revealing the relative number and size of the older, larger-than-average bucks (i.e., trophies) and the top-end size possible in the area. In a lightly hunted herd, the relative trophy prospects are excellent, as revealed by the graph. The trophy prospects are diminished but reasonable in a moderately hunted herd. In heavily hunted herds, trophy prospects are pretty much limited to the outside hope of killing any mature buck, most likely a 3½.

ILLUSTRATING PLACE TO PLACE COMPARISONS

When the relative trophy prospects are considered across the continent, the very real size differences from place to place become major considerations. This is where genetics and nutrition enter the picture...and, as taxonomists would say, the subspecies differences. Whatever the reason, great differences in the size of bucks, even those of the same age, exist from region to region across the country. For the traveling hunter interested in hunting the biggest bucks available, this is an important factor in his analysis of trophy prospects. Once again, a graph will best illustrate these dramatic regional size differences. For the sake of comparison, let's look at three different herds—one with inherently small deer, one with average-sized deer and one with large deer—and eliminate any age differences by assuming they are all subjected to the same moderate hunting pressure (see graph on next page).

If you're interested in shooting the biggest deer possible, where would you go? To the "large deer" region, of course! If your trophy goal is a 150, just compare the height of the curves at that point on the size line. There is virtually no

INHERENT SIZE DIFFERENCES FROM PLACE TO PLACE

How genetics and nutrition yield the size of bucks under the same hunting pressure in three different regions.

GROSS B&C SCORE OF MATURE BUCKS

hope of shooting such a buck in the "small deer" region and only a very slim chance of doing it in the "average deer" region. But, the large deer region . . . ah, you've got a running chance to find a 150-class buck there.

PUTTING IT ALL TOGETHER

From what we've just seen, it is possible, given enough information about hunting pressure and buck size, to develop graphs painting a fairly accurate picture of trophy prospects for a particular place or region. Let's turn back to the two settings—middle Georgia and northwest Montana—used in the opening of this chapter. A graph combining the effects of hunting pressure and inherent buck size will graphically illustrate the difference in the trophy prospects in these two areas and demonstrate how such graphs can be used to "picture" the comparative trophy prospects across the continent, which we will do later.

This graph reflects the telling impact of hunting pressure and overcrowding even more than the genetic differences in buck size between the two regions. While Montana bucks

COMPARATIVE TROPHY PROSPECTS BETWEEN MIDDLE GEORGIA AND NORTHWEST MONTANA

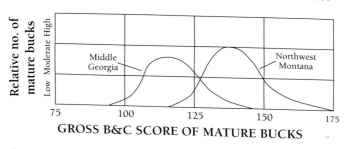

do have a genetic edge for size over middle Georgia bucks, that difference is not as great as one might think, owing in part to the fact the middle Georgia herd is permeated with genes from the inherently large Wisconsin deer stocked in Georgia during the 1950s and 60s. The real difference between the two curves lies in the fact that Georgia has too many deer (resulting in poor nutrition that limits full realization of the genetic potential at any given age) and is subject to much more pressure (limiting age structure) than Montana.

Pressure in Montana is light by any standards. The only reason the number of mature bucks reflected on the graph is not higher is because the deer population in northwest Montana is relatively low, at least compared to Georgia's. The age structure, however, is excellent, resulting in plenty of older age-class bucks (5½ to 7½) and excellent trophy hunting.

In middle Georgia, pressure borders on high because of the close proximity of Atlanta. The high deer population there is the only reason the number of mature bucks creeps into the moderate range. The vast majority of the mature bucks taken are 3½ years old. A few 4½s show up, but 5½s are downright scarce, which curtails top-end size.

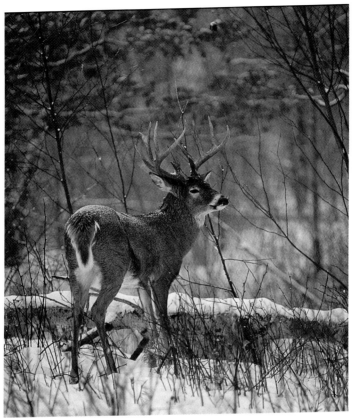

Huntability varies from region to region. This usually means vegetation and terrain, but weather is definitely a factor. Cold and snow are usually favorable—but only if you can stand it!

As the graph shows, the "average" mature buck in middle Georgia grosses about 115, as opposed to 135 in northwest Montana. In Georgia, a 125 is a fine trophy, but it takes something close to 150 to rank trophy status in Montana. Such a buck is pretty much a pipe dream in Georgia, although the odd one does show up occasionally. A 160s buck is by no means out of the question in northwest Montana. In fact, several Boone & Crocketts are shot there every year. In the 20 years I hunted middle Georgia, I averaged a 130 or better every year or two and managed to kill two 150-class bucks . . . and that was with hard hunting on a far better-than-average place. By contrast, I've either killed or passed up 150-class bucks each of the three years I've lived and hunted in northwest Montana . . . without hunting any harder or smarter than I did those 20 years in Georgia!

To complete the picture, a word about huntability is needed. As we've seen, huntability depends on two major factors—habitat conditions and hunting pressure. Middle Georgia, with its broken country, abundant edge and well-defined food sources, is definitely easier to hunt than northwest Montana, where vast, unbroken forest and rough terrain characterize much of its habitat. However, much higher pressure in Georgia has adversely affected herd structure and normal activity patterns and largely off-set any advantage over Montana gained by virtue of more huntable habitat. The net result, then, is that the huntability of the two places is about the same. Thus, the graph does indeed reflect an accurate comparison of the relative trophy prospects in Montana versus that of Georgia, which explains in part why I now live in Montana!

CHAPTER FOUR

TROPHY PROSPECTS ACROSS NORTH AMERICA

The whitetail is truly a remarkable animal. Its great intelligence and adaptability have made it the most abundant big game animal in North America. In fact, at 20 million strong, the whitetail may well be the most abundant big game animal on earth! Yet, despite its numbers and an annual harvest of over four million, a trophy whitetail still stands as one of hunting's greatest challenges and most treasured prizes. As we've seen, if you want to be counted among the fortunate few who take true trophies with any consistency, you have to hunt where such trophies live in appreciable numbers. In this chapter and the one to follow, we're going to try to identify those places.

Our survey will begin with a sweep across the continent using the Boone & Crockett records to look at where the very biggest bucks hail from. This will tell us much, but certainly not all, about where trophies are found. We will get a good idea which states and provinces have the greatest top-end potential, but that won't always translate into the place that offers the best chance of shooting a trophy under our definition. Also, the number of book deer officially recorded does not always accurately reflect either the number of record bucks that have been killed there or the relative number currently living there. For instance, a comparatively small percentage of the book bucks shot in the

Canadian provinces are ever entered in the Boone & Crockett records. In tradition-rich states like Wisconsin and Minnesota, where big buck shows and programs have been underway for years, few book deer go unrecognized.

Also, in states or provinces where hunting pressure is very low, as is the case in the Northwest, British Columbia, and Canada's Maritime provinces, the number of bucks listed does not provide a good means of comparison to more heavily hunted areas. You see, where pressure is light, the record buck tally is achieved through harvesting a lower percentage of the available trophy bucks, leaving plenty of big bucks to carry over to next year. On the other hand, a heavily-hunted place will see a much higher percentage of its big bucks shot each year and fewer carried over to provide good trophy hunting the following year. For instance, New Brunswick and Mississippi both have about 25 bucks currently listed, but lightly hunted New Brunswick has achieved that number with far less pressure and has record bucks dying of old age there every year. Much heavier-hunted Mississippi, on the other hand, has laid claim to its 25 B&Cs by mounting enough pressure to account for darn near every record buck that walks that fine deer state in any given year. You, the trophy hunter, can't hope to draw a bead on bucks that have already been shot; you need bucks that are still in the woods walking around.

Still, we can learn much from what the record books can tell us. After all, a record buck is at the very top of the size pyramid, and for every book buck listed, many other great trophy bucks that fall short of the record are taken by hunters in that state or province. This fact alone dictates that we pay close attention to what the record book tells us. (Note: All B&C data was compiled by Dave Boland from the 10th Edition (1993) of Boone & Crockett's *Records Of North American Big Game*.)

Where The All-Time B&C Bucks Were Taken

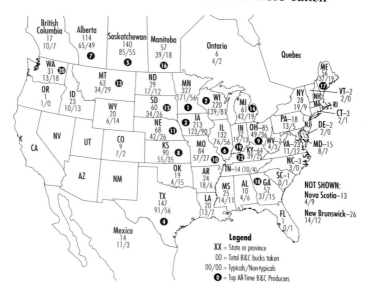

Legend
XX = State or province
00 = Total B&C bucks taken
00/00 = Typicals/Non-typicals
❶ = Top All-Time B&C Producers

NOT SHOWN:
Nova Scotia—13
4/9

New Brunswick—26
14/12

Minnesota, with its 327 book bucks, is firmly ensconced at the head of the overall record book list. Wisconsin is second with 220, but I don't look for Wisconsin to hold the runner up position much longer. Iowa, No.3 with 213, has closed to within seven of Wisconsin thanks to a dominating run of 130 new entries since 1980! During that same time, Wisconsin added 81. But regardless of the order of the ranking, the tri-state area of Minnesota, Wisconsin and Iowa have accounted for 760 record bucks, an amazing 31 percent of the all-time total across the entire continent! Considering the United States only, these three states claim an overwhelming 36 percent of the record book! While both Minnesota and Wisconsin continue to produce lots of Boone and Crocketts, hunting pressure has cut into their potential. Iowa, Kansas and Illinois, however, have less

THE TOP 20 RECENT PRODUCERS (1980-1991)

	Location	No. Bucks		Location	No. Bucks
1.	Iowa	130	11.	Michigan	31
2.	Minnesota	112	12.	Manitoba	29
3.	Illinois	95	13.	Texas	28
4.	Wisconsin	81	14.	Georgia	26
5.	Kansas	70	15.	Indiana	25
6.	Alberta	62	16.	Nebraska	21
7.	Missouri	50	17.	Maine	21
8.	Ohio	48	18.	Montana	17
9.	Kentucky	43	19.	Oklahoma	14
10.	Saskatchewan	41	20.	Mississippi	14

WHERE THE GIANTS CALL HOME

Typicals (Bucks over 190)				Non-Typicals (Bucks over 245)			
	Location	No.	Biggest		Location	No.	Biggest
1.	Iowa	9	201 4/8	1.	Minnesota	7	268 5/8
2.	Minnesota	8	202 0/8	2.	Iowa	6	282 0/8
3.	Saskatch.	7	200 2/8	3.	Kansas	5	269 3/8
4.	Texas	5	196 4/8	4.	Ohio	4	328 2/8
5.	Wisconsin	4	206 1/8	5.	Saskatch.	4	267 7/8
6.	Illinois	4	204 4/8	6.	Texas	3	286 0/8
7.	Missouri	3	205 0/8	7.	Alberta	3	279 6/8
8.	Kansas	3	198 2/8	8.	Idaho	3	268 0/8
9.	Nebraska	3	199 2/8	9.	S. Dakota	3	256 1/8
10.	Indiana	3	195 1/8	10.	Missouri	2	333 7/8
11.	Alberta	2	204 2/8	11.	Nova Scotia	2	273 6/8
12.	Montana	2	199 3/8	12.	Montana	2	252 1/8
13.	S. Dakota	2	193 0/8	13.	Maine	2	248 1/8
14.	Ohio	1	201 1/8	14.	Nebraska	1	277 3/8
15.	New York	1	198 3/8	15.	Illinois	1	267 3/8
16.	Manitoba	1	197 7/8	16.	Alabama	1	259 7/8
17.	Michigan	1	193 2/8	17.	Manitoba	1	257 3/8
18.	Maine	1	192 7/8	18.	N. Dakota	1	254 6/8
19.	Wyoming	1	191 5/8	19.	N. Brunswick	1	249 7/8
20.	Kentucky	1	191 3/8	20.	Virginia	1	249 3/8
				21.	Indiana	1	248 4/8
				22.	Oklahoma	1	247 7/8
				23.	B. Columbia	1	245 7/8
				24.	Wisconsin	1	245 0/8

Few hunters are optimistic enough to seriously search for the one-in-several hundred thousand Boone & Crockett buck—but historic numbers of record heads indicates a much greater number of nice, trophy-class bucks.

pressure, owing in part to restrictive seasons, and are now posting very impressive numbers. A look at "The Top 20 Recent Producers" will tell the story since 1980: Iowa, 130; Minnesota, 112; Illinois, 95; Wisconsin, 81; and Kansas, 70. Throw in the neighboring states of Nebraska, Missouri, Indiana, Michigan and Ohio and you've pretty well defined the hotbed of B&C production in the U.S.

Texas stands as an anomaly in the world of record whitetails, especially when you consider that most of its 147 record bucks came from subtropical South Texas. The general trend is for buck size to increase with latitude, but Texas defies that trend and ranks as the No.4 all-time B&C

producer, although I expect that position to be yielded in the next few years.

Georgia is also a bit of a trend-breaker. Its 52 record bucks completely overshadow the totals of the other Deep South states. Why is that so? Almost certainly because of the successful stocking of Wisconsin deer into vacant habitat during the restoration years of the 1950s and 60s. Genetics do make a difference! Also, Ohio and Kentucky both stand out compared to their immediate neighbors.

More than any other place in the U.S., the B&C numbers probably do not accurately represent the trophy prospects in the northwestern states of Montana, Idaho and Washington. Even today, many of the record bucks killed there never make their way to the hallowed halls of Boone & Crockett. For instance, I personally knew of nine B&Cs killed in northwest Montana during a single season a few years ago. Only three of them were reported. Many unscored B&C contenders are hanging in service stations, bars and certainly in homes throughout the Northwest. Additionally, low hunting pressure in these states hold down the number of record bucks harvested there each year in proportion to what is actually walking around there.

If the B&C totals don't really tell the story for the Northwest, that goes in spades in Canada. Saskatchewan only has 140 to its credit, but the best estimates say that the province produces over 40 book deer a year. One provincial record-keeping organization has over 400 possible B&C bucks listed! Saskatchewan's trophy potential was broadcast loud and clear in 1993 when Milo Hanson of Biggar, Saskatchewan, shot a typical 12-pointer scoring 213⅛. This deer broke a 30-year record to become the new world record. I consider Saskatchewan to be the No.1

place on the continent for record-class bucks. Alberta is not far behind! Also, the prime whitetail country in Manitoba compares favorably with that of Saskatchewan and Alberta, but there's not nearly as much of it.

It is interesting to note the strong tendency toward non-typicals in the northwestern U.S. Non-typicals actually outnumber typicals in Wyoming, Idaho and Washington and almost equal typicals in Montana. Apparently, this area has a genetic disposition for non-typicals. The Canadian Maritime Provinces of New Brunswick and Nova Scotia also have a disproportionate ratio of non-typicals, as do Alabama and Virginia. For sheer numbers, however, the Midwest and central Canada have the edge even for non-typicals.

"The Top 20 Recent Producers" listing offers a couple of interesting insights. First, it's no surprise that the Midwest and Central Canada account for all the top 10 entries . . . all, that is, except for Kentucky. With 43 recent entries, Kentucky stacks up well against some pretty illustrious company—only five behind Ohio and seven behind Missouri but ahead of such notables as Saskatchewan, Michigan, Manitoba and Texas. Also noteworthy is Indiana, where 25 of its all-time total of 32 record bucks have come since 1980. If there is another surprise, at least to me, it is that Kansas comes in fifth with only 70 book deer since 1980. I would have thought this great trophy state would have fared better.

In the "Where The Giants Call Home" listing, only Texas interrupts the dominance of the Midwest and Central Canada in both the typical and non-typical rankings. Also of interest, although Ohio only has one typical topping 190, it has yielded four giant non-typicals. With three giant typicals and five non-typicals, Kansas shows why it has a

The famed "Hole-In-The-Horn" buck was found dead in Ohio, a state that has produced an inordinate number of big non-typicals.

growing reputation for world-class bucks. The overwhelm-ing strength of Minnesota and Iowa is evident. Area for area, Iowa undoubtedly harbors more B&C bucks today than any other place in the U.S. and even rivals any like area in central Canada!

CHAPTER FIVE

REGION-BY-REGION
TROPHY PROSPECTS

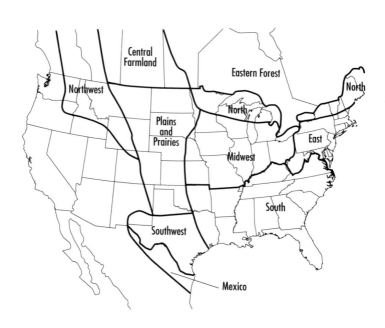

In this chapter, we'll divide North America into regions based on similarity of habitat, current trophy prospects, geographic location and hunting traditions. Then, we'll explore the trophy prospects in each region by employing the graph we developed earlier. Obviously, our survey will be no more than a general stereotyping of what to expect within the region. The quality of trophy hunting can and does vary greatly within any given region, and we cannot possibly deal with the many exceptions.

Keep in mind that we are considering only mature bucks, i.e., those 3½ years old and older. Also, remember that our definition of a trophy is a mature buck big enough to be among the best consistently taken in a given area.

One last note. The following graphs represent somewhat better than average trophy prospects for each region. The reason for this is that a trophy hunter is going to put forth an effort to search out a place where his chances are better than those of the masses. I chose to do this after looking at some worst case scenarios and across-the-board averages. In some instances, what I saw would discourage even the most enthusiastic would-be trophy hunter.

NORTH REGION

Relative no. of mature bucks — Low Moderate High

75   100   125   150   175

GROSS B&C SCORE OF MATURE BUCKS

The legendary North Country, a harsh land of cold, snow and deep evergreen forest, is steeped in deer hunting traditon. Names like the Upper Peninsula, Adirondack Mountains and, yes, even Maine, Wisconsin and Minnesota all bring images of big bucks tracking through fresh snow to true whitetail aficionados. Despite its fame, hunting in the North Country is not easy. Lots of snow, extreme cold, rugged terrain, vast, unbroken woods and low deer densities in many areas make hunting there among the hardest anywhere, but some of the biggest bucks in the country could be the payoff.

Even though pressure in this region ranges from moderate in the southern reaches to low in the northern locales, the number of mature bucks is relatively low simply because deer densities are so low. An excellent buck age structure, especially in the wilder areas, pushes the average mature buck score up to about 135. Difficult hunting conditions and low numbers make a 140 a trophy, but every year, 160-plus bucks are killed there. This region has the big deer; the problem is killing them. An aggressive, physically fit hunter has a definite edge when it comes to consistently ferreting out big bucks in this challenging land.

Part of the mystique of the North Country is the expectation that something huge can walk out at anytime. Indeed, a number of book deer are shot in the better areas of the region every year and some are real whoppers. In Minnesota and Wisconsin particularly, the trophy potential is world class, as the record book will attest. Northern Maine, New Brunswick, and Nova Scotia, all of which are poured from the same mold, have a well-deserved reputation for huge bucks. Northern New York, Vermont and New Hampshire have some good bucks but don't have the top-end size of the other areas in the region. Upper Michigan's top-end falls somewhere in the middle.

Much of the East holds relatively little promise for the serious trophy hunter. The reason is simple—hunting

THE EAST

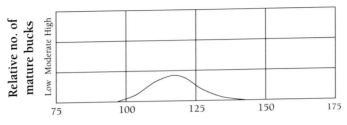

GROSS B&C SCORE OF MATURE BUCKS

pressure. Few bucks live long enough to achieve any size. Even 3½s are scarce in the heaviest hunted places, and anything older is rarer than an honest fisherman. This is shown on the graph by the limited size range (100 to 130) and the low number of mature bucks, practically all of which are 3½s. As you can see, the top-end is seriously curtailed. A 140 would gather a crowd almost anywhere there.

Interestingly, some of the better bucks in the East are in suburban areas where hunting is restricted or off-limits. Good bucks live in the small, neighborhood woodlots in Connecticut, Massachusetts, Rhode Island and even New Jersey. Since hunters don't generally have access to them (except for a few bowhunters), those deer are not considered in a discussion of trophy prospects. Of the places available to hunters, the less pressured areas of West Virginia, Vermont and New Hampshire and some of the larger, protected farms in Maryland and southern Pennsylvania offer pretty good hunting for bucks in the 120 to 135 range. But, this quality is not the norm for the region.

Overall, the average size of the relatively few bucks that make it to maturity is around 115, but that doesn't reflect the true size potential, even considering that they're nearly all 3½s. Overcrowding has long been a problem and has drastically cut into buck size. Perhaps even more insidious is the erosion of genetic quality in certain areas due to the near total harvest of bucks with clearly visible antlers, leaving only the smallest bucks to do the breeding.

Even though huntability is fairly good in the East, it doesn't help much when mature bucks are so few and far between. The serious trophy hunter there has to seek out the more remote, unhunted areas or protected private land to have consistent success.

THE SOUTH

GROSS B&C SCORE OF MATURE BUCKS

The tradition of hunting runs deep in the South. High deer densities, long seasons, liberal bag limits and a large rural population make deer hunting an important part of Southern culture. The South is a diverse region; habitats vary from rugged mountains to vast river swamps to gently rolling hills of broken forests to flat, monoculture piney-woods. Most hunting is done on private land, and trophy management of varying levels is on a rapid rise throughout the South. As a result of all this, the amount of hunting pressure differs greatly from one area to another and even from one tract to another.

Overall, pressure leans to the high side of moderate in the South, thus the number of mature bucks is low-moderate

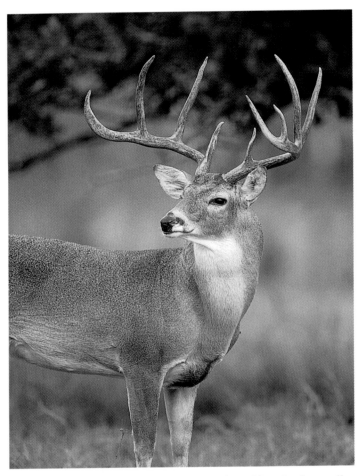

Texas, especially South Texas is an anomaly; although of a smaller subspecies, the best Texas bucks grow amazing antlers. In general, though, the larger-bodied the deer the better the antler potential.

even though deer densities are high. In recent years, the cumulative detrimental effect of overcrowding may well have surpassed even the lack of age as the greatest limiting factor in antler size. In large areas of the South, the habitat has been scoured by too many deer for years and now the nutrition necessary to produce quality antlers is simply not there. As a result of the lack of age and good nutrition, the average size of mature bucks in the South is about 110. Trophy status starts at 120, and anything over 130 is exceptional. Though bigger ones are killed there, a 140 is pretty much the realistic top-end. It was not always that way, however.

During the 1970s and early 80s on the middle Georgia property I hunted, 3½-year-old bucks commonly scored 125 to 135 and a 4½ or better was sure to crowd or top 140. On that same property today, most 3½s score 100 to 115 and even the occasional 4½ seldom breaks 130 ... all because too many mouths have been out there for too many years. That's unfortunate because the management potential to produce quality deer in the South is tremendous . . . if hunters will restrain their trigger finger on young bucks and take enough does to keep the herd in check. Of course, the game departments must provide regulations that will allow enough does to be taken, which they haven't always done. On the positive side, the South has tremendous recuperative powers with its warm climate and long growing season so it is possible to quickly remedy the ills of the past.

As for huntability, the South has to be slightly harder than average to hunt. Thick, leafy cover adds an element of difficulty to hunting. Hunting pressure, worsened in areas by dog hunting and very long seasons, causes deer to move mostly at first and last light, or at night. Even the typically warm weather encourages nocturnal movement. Without food plots or agriculture to expose and concentrate deer, the South can prove to be a fairly difficult place to hunt.

THE MIDWEST

Relative no. of mature bucks — Low Moderate High

75   100   125   150   175

GROSS B&C SCORE OF MATURE BUCKS

The Midwest, with expansive fields of corn, soybeans and small grain, produces some of the biggest bucks on the continent. Superior genetics, fertile soils, and a great abundance of nutritious food are the reasons. Since cover, not food, is the limiting factor, deer populations vary according to available cover. Fair to good numbers exist where cover is in sufficient supply.

Overall, pressure is moderate, but some areas are subjected to heavy pressure. Hunting pressure has taken a toll on the number and age of the mature bucks in some areas, but enough bucks live long enough to provide some of the finest giant buck hunting to be found.

Because of limited cover, the Midwest offers high huntability. Besides the Plains & Prairies Region, which in many respects is very similar, I consider the Midwest to be perhaps the most huntable of all regions, at least when it comes to hunting an individual buck once he's located. Well-defined food sources, clear travel corridors and limited bedding options make patterning a buck fairly easy. However, hunting the Midwest is not without its obstacles.

One of the main difficulties is that hunting is mostly on small tracts of land, usually from 150 to 500 acres, and bucks may spend only part of their time on any given tract.

The Plains and Prairies region not only produces superb whitetails, but is perhaps the most huntable of all regions.

This can limit access to big bucks and make patterning difficult. Also, short seasons, weapons restrictions and, in some cases, limited firearms seasons during the peak of rut act to swing the odds back in the buck's favor. All this means that seeing a big buck in the Midwest is not necessarily the problem; killing him may be.

As the graph shows, the average mature buck in the Midwest scores an impressive 140 or so. There are plenty of 150s around, and 160s are a distinct possibility. Record book bucks are there in numbers only Central Canada can match. Still, big bucks are not everywhere even in the Midwest. They are widely scattered among the many small farms, and unless you know there's a big buck on the tract you're hunting, the Midwest can be frustrating. For the serious hunter willing to do his homework and find a specific buck to hunt, there is absolutely no better place to shoot a 160-plus buck, or even a book deer for that matter. But because of the need to hunt a specific farm, as opposed to an area, and preferably even a specific buck, the resident hunter has a great advantage over the visiting hunter in the Midwest.

THE PLAINS & PRAIRIES

Relative no. of mature bucks — Low Moderate High

75   100   125   150   175

GROSS B&C SCORE OF MATURE BUCKS

Depending on where you are in the region, you may know the Plains & Prairies for its endless wheat fields or shimmering grasslands or perhaps its stark sagebrush-studded landscape. To the Eastern hunter, this country doesn't look much like a place harboring big whitetails, but the fact is that the Plains & Prairies Region is one of the better trophy areas in the U.S.

This region is unique in that its whitetail populations are largely confined to ribbons of habitat, namely riverbottoms and the fingers of cover radiating off them. Often, fertile agricultural fields are adjacent to the riverbottoms to provide an abundant food source for the deer. Along these watercourses, deer densities can be among the highest anywhere and overcrowding is a problem in many areas. Yet, vast chunks of this region have few or no whitetails. The Plains & Prairies curve only reflects the riverbottom habitat.

The Plains & Prairies is one of the most huntable regions since the deer are largely confined to strips of cover. This is ranch country, and pressure, herd condition and habitat quality vary considerably from ranch to ranch. Overall, pressure is low to low-moderate, but even at that, high huntability has generally reduced the number of mature bucks present and the top-end size. Still, low pressure and high deer densities result in one of the highest localized populations of mature bucks to be found. For sheer numbers of mature bucks, only the famed ranches of Texas can compare with the better Plains & Prairie ranches.

The average mature buck scores around 130, and anything over 140 is a trophy. Bucks topping 150 are in fair abundance on the better ranches, and 160s are there but take some hard looking. Despite some slippage in top-end size, book deer are shot there every year. Overall, the Plains & Prairies is one of the very best places to tag a 125 to 150-class whitetail. I actually rank the better ranches there on par with the better ranches in South Texas, and where overcrowding is not a problem and hunting pressure is minimal, the top-end can be even better!

THE NORTHWEST

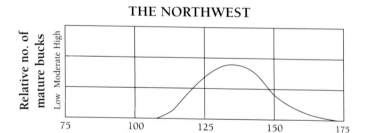

GROSS B&C SCORE OF MATURE BUCKS

In this vast mountainous country, the bugle of the elk fills the autumn mornings, the grizzly still roams the backcountry, moose forage the hidden beaver ponds, mule deer feed in the Alpine meadows and the buffalo still roams . . . right alongside big whitetails. This the land of the great Rocky Mountains, and many of the valleys and associated hillsides are home to the whitetail.

I have chosen to combine both the Canadian and the U.S. Rockies in this region because the trophy prospects north and south of the border are essentially the same. Only the eastern front of the Alberta Rockies, where massive bucks typical of farmland Canada are sometimes shot, edges ahead of the overall trophy prospects of the rest of the region. Also, hunting quality tends to tail off as you move farther west into British Columbia and Washington and Oregon.

Hunting pressure is fairly low throughout the region, and on average, deer populations are moderate, which is why the number of mature bucks on the graph is only shown as moderate. The average mature buck runs a very respectable 135. Bucks in the 150s are present in encouraging numbers, and I consider this size buck to be an achievable goal for the serious trophy hunter with a week or so to spare during the rut. A 160-plus is a realistic possibility, and record bucks are not uncommon. With the vast public holdings on the U.S. side, this area offers the best public land hunting for trophy whitetails in the country.

The one drawback in this region is its huntability. The expansive evergreen forests are not easy to hunt, especially for those new to the region. Deer populations tend to be somewhat localized, and figuring out what the deer are doing can be an intimidating experience when someone first tackles this rugged, inaccessible and sometimes inhospitable country. Only the Eastern Forest Region of Canada and the North Region would be harder to hunt than the Northwest, but higher deer populations and lower hunting pressure make hunter success much higher in the Northwest.

In the Southwest Region, we're only going to focus on the two main areas: the Texas Hill Country and South Texas Brush Country, two of the most remarkable deer areas in the world! The graph will clearly show why these two places are among the most popular destination points for traveling whitetail hunters on the continent. They both have some of the highest numbers of mature bucks found

THE SOUTHWEST

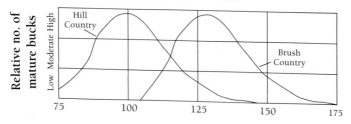

GROSS B&C SCORE OF MATURE BUCKS

anywhere, although the size of the bucks differs greatly between the two areas. Only the riverbottoms of the Plains & Prairies Region can compare with the Hill Country and Brush Country for sheer numbers of mature bucks.

The quality of hunting in general and trophy hunting in particular varies tremendously within both the Hill Country and Brush Country. The reason for this is deer management. Many ranches practice some of the most intense trophy management in the world, including in many cases the use of game-proof fences to control the herd. Others have more modest programs that limit harvests and promote quality to varying degrees. Some places have no management at all and have depleted buck populations. The graph depicts ranches with above average management programs to reflect the recognized potential of the region. Interestingly, I know of nowhere else that buck size varies so much within such close proximity as does that of the Hill Country and Brush Country.

The graph reflects the Hill Country's very high number of mature bucks, even though pressure there is moderate. This is because the Hill Country has the highest concentration of whitetails in the world! It has been estimated that 10 percent of all the whitetails in North America live in the Hill Country! Deer densities run from 40 to an incredible

100 per square mile. Unfortunately, all these mouths to feed has taken a toll on buck size there.

While the average mature buck in the Hill Country scores no more than 100, their overwhelming abundance results in a good supply of bucks up to 115 or so. A 120 is a mighty fine Hill Country buck. A 130 is most exceptional on all but the most intensively managed ranches. The reasonable top-end is about 140. But to show what the Hill Country is capable of when the herd is held in check, the harvest tightly controlled and a quality food supply maintained, I have a friend who intensively manages a 1,200-acre high-fenced ranch that has produced several bucks topping 150 and a couple well into the 160s over the last half-dozen years. Overall, however, I consider the Hill Country to be the best place on the continent to shoot a buck scoring from 90 to 120.

The Hill Country is highly huntable. While there are places with impenetrable stands of cedar and rugged terrain, much of the Hill Country consists of reasonably open live oak stands interspersed with grassy meadows. The hills themselves offer good vantage points for extended visibility. Additionally, these small Texas deer tend to move freely during daylight hours. The fact that baiting is legal and widely practiced doesn't hurt huntability, either.

For the serious trophy hunter, South Texas is one of the premier trophy spots in North America. South Texas is an arid, semi-tropical land covered with thorny brush that at first glance doesn't look like it would support an anorexic rabbit. But is that ever a wrong impression!

On the graph, the first thing you'll notice is the extraordinary number and size of mature bucks in South Texas. A combination of factors contribute to this remarkable situation. One, the region consists largely of expansive ranches, many 10,000 to 25,000 acres and some more than

100,000 acres, that are closely protected and managed. Two, the soil is very fertile, thus the scraggly-looking plants are deceptively nutritious. Three, the genetic potential for big racks is excellent, which is surprising given the extreme southern location. Four, although the region supports a high deer population, periodic droughts and heavy predation, especially on fawns, tend to serve as a built-in mechanism to prevent overcrowding. As a result, relatively unhunted herds can stay in balance with their habitat, which allows for the virtual stockpiling of older, bigger bucks. All these things make South Texas most unique ... and the No.1 place in the world to shoot a buck scoring between 120 and 150!

Hunting pressure in South Texas is low, and the harvest there is the most selective anywhere. Hunters are looking for something special and seldom shoot the first buck to come along. Few immature bucks are taken if any type of management is in place. As a result, the effective hunting pressure is even lower than the actual hunter-days applied. This makes for a very high population of mature bucks.

As the graph shows, the average mature buck in the Brush Country pushes 130, owing to the high average age. There are plenty of 140s around. Though 150-plus bucks are starting to represent a relatively small percentage of mature bucks, the sheer number of mature bucks present results in an abundance of 150s, rivaling even the giant buck regions of the Midwest and Central Canada. As you move into the 160s, South Texas starts to lag behind the Midwest and Central Canada but is still in the game. When it comes to book deer, South Texas doesn't stack up nearly as well either in terms of actual numbers or percentage of the buck kill. Still, South Texas does turn out several book deer a year, provided the rains hit right, among its whitetail harvest of about 450,000. For my money, the best ranches in

South Texas offer the finest trophy whitetail hunting experience on earth!

Huntability varies considerably in South Texas. In the eastern coastal areas, the deer are perhaps the most naive and vulnerable anywhere. Living among live oak mottes scattered throughout open grasslands, the deer are not only highly visible but for reasons I don't fully understand they are exceptionally tame for a whitetail. As you move farther west into the more classic Brush Country, not only is the cover thicker but the deer are wilder. By the time you get to the western edge of the Brush Country near the Rio Grande, the thorn brush is wall-to-wall and the bucks are spring-loaded bundles of nerves. Overall huntability in the Brush Country ranks somewhere in the middle of the spectrum . . . except during the rut, when huntability becomes better than average because of the high competition between the many mature bucks.

MEXICO

GROSS B&C SCORE OF MATURE BUCKS

In Mexico, we're only going to concern ourselves with the area along the Rio Grande adjacent to Texas. As expected, this region is basically an extension of South Texas except that the land and the deer herds have been exploited more. As a result, the quality of the deer habitat and deer populations vary greatly. Even more so than in

South Texas, the trophy prospects in Mexico boil down to individual ranches.

Even on the better ranches, deer populations tend to run lower than in South Texas. The reason for this is twofold. One, the range has been grazed heavier by livestock and does not support as many deer. Two, poaching has been a long-standing problem. But there is some good in all this. Since overcrowding is not a problem, bucks can reach impressive size if they live long enough. While Mexico does not have nearly as many mature bucks as South Texas, as the graph illustrates, the average size is at least as large. Heavier mass seems to be a common characteristic of the top-end bucks.

Like South Texas, mature bucks in Mexico will average around 135. Bucks in the 140s are generally considered good there, but serious trophy hunters shoot for something in the 150s. Hard hunting and time can yield 160-plus bucks on the best ranches, but at that point, you're playing some pretty long odds. Yet, the top-end there is surprisingly strong, and Mexico offers an element of mystery since you never know what might walk out.

CENTRAL CANADA

GROSS B&C SCORE OF MATURE BUCKS

Central Canada is a frigid, snow-covered land where the arena for a trophy hunt can be either great northern forests or small woodlots dotting expansive agricultural fields. The deer there are perhaps the biggest of the species. Low to moderate pressure, especially in "big bush" areas along the northern fringes of the farm country, allows many bucks to reach the necessary age to realize their great size potential. Harsh winters and predation from coyotes and wolves act to prevent overcrowding. In fact, deer populations are moderate at best and are downright low in many areas. Low deer densities coupled with poor logistics, restrictive laws, extreme cold and deer that lean toward nocturnal activity make Central Canada a challenging place to hunt.

The moderate number of mature bucks reflected in the graph is because deer populations are only moderate at best. Though pressure tends to be low to moderate overall, some of the more southern farm country gets hammered pretty hard, making mature bucks hard to find there. The number of mature bucks increases as pressure decreases and cover increases in the northern fringe country, where most nonresidents are forced to hunt by law.

You would think these farm country bucks would be fairly easy to hunt, but that is not the case. They are very skittish and tend to be nocturnal. Also, they often cover long distances in their travels, especially during the rut, making locating even a known buck rather dicey. Interestingly, their big woods counterparts in the northern forests areas are much more apt to move around in daylight and are less skittish.

In areas where baiting is legal and practiced, namely upper Saskatchewan, I would describe huntability as fair. I can't rank it much better than that because the harsh weather and often poor logistics still make hunting very tough. Plus, mature bucks are not as easy to bait in as some would have you believe. Where baiting is not legal in

Alberta and Manitoba, huntability is something less than fair, especially outside the rut. Limited daytime movement often requires that deer drives be employed.

On average, mature bucks score a whopping 140-plus in Central Canada. They routinely top 150. Scores in the 160s are common for older age-class bucks, i.e., 5½ and older. Record-class bucks are an ever-present possibility. In fact, I'm certain that a higher percentage of the mature bucks reach record-class there than anywhere else in the world. The top-end is virtually unlimited, and world-class bucks are shot there every year. The only area that even compares to Central Canada is the Midwest. No other place consistently turns out such massive antlers as this region. For giant whitetails, those over 160, I consider this region to be the best place going for the visiting hunter. (Resident Midwest hunters may have just as good a chance at home.) But, big bucks do not come easy in Central Canada, so be prepared to return home empty-handed if you go there.

EASTERN CANADA

GROSS B&C SCORE OF MATURE BUCKS

This region consists largely of vast, wilderness forests more suited to moose than whitetails. Most deer are found where man's activities, namely farming, clearing and timbering, have replaced the comparatively sterile virgin forests with crops or regrowth that make life in the harsh land more bearable for the whitetail. The best deer hunting is around the scattered pockets of agriculture, found mostly along the U.S. border.

Deer numbers there range from fair around the border agricultural areas to downright disparaging in the remoter, less disturbed areas. For our purposes, we're only going to consider the areas along the border that have reasonable populations of deer. Happily, hunting pressure is light almost everywhere. Even at that, the number of mature bucks on our graph is still relatively low simply because deer densities are meager.

For reasons I've never fully understood, deer in this region do not reach the antler size (body sizes can be impressive there) of their U.S. counterparts just across the border. It must be a combination of the soils, genetics and perhaps weather, which is characterized by severe cold and deep snow. As you move farther east into the Maritime provinces, trophy size does increase once again, especially antler mass.

As the graph shows, mature bucks average about 120. A 130 is a trophy. Only in the best agricultural areas are bucks topping 140 a reasonable hope. A 150-class buck is about as big as you can expect. But as the record book shows, Ontario has squeezed out six book bucks, so the region can hold a surprise or two.

Huntability depends on where you are in the region. In the big bush areas, finding a buck, let alone a trophy, can be more work and challenge than most hunters care to take on. In the farming areas, huntability can be fair to good, depending on the layout of the land and on hunting pressure. On balance, this is a difficult region to hunt. Couple that with low deer populations and limited size potential, and you can see why this region has captured little of the trophy hunting limelight.

CHAPTER SIX

THE BIG PICTURE

Many deer hunters fail to realize that deer follow distinct and predictable activity patterns in the fall. As fall progresses, major movement and behavioral changes occur, yet too often hunters never adapt to these changes. Some hunters will scout around opening weekend and, after finding some sign, set up to hunt that site. Then, as days and even weeks pass, they continue to hunt that same spot, even though the deer changed their pattern long ago and the sign has dried up. The truth is the savvy hunter doesn't even have to depend on sign. He actually can predict the changes before they occur . . . if he understands seasonal movement patterns and how to react to them. That's exactly what we're going to try to figure out in this section of the book. But first, some preliminaries.

A deer's seasonal biological clock is controlled by the length of day. This is called photoperiodism. The timing of changes triggered by daylength is almost exactly the same from year to year in a given place. Obviously, some deer will precede the majority and some will trail, but the peak activity, which we're interested in, will occur on a predictable timetable. Once you know when certain activities have occurred historically in your area, predicting their arrival is an easy matter, barring major changes in the herd.

Although the timing, duration and exact nature of patterns are consistent from year to year in any given area,

Understanding the changing behavior and patterns of the whitetail during the fall is absolutely critical to big buck success. This 155-class buck was taken on a pre-rut feeding pattern after several days of hunting him.

considerable differences exist from region to region. Hunting pressure, latitude, physical condition of the deer, herd density, habitat type, and terrain are all important factors influencing when and how patterns are played out in the various regions. Even on a localized basis, the combined effects of hunting pressure, weather and other factors may alter patterns, sign and activity from what we describe as "normal." In our discussion, we will be looking at the ideal.

For whitetails and whitetail hunters alike, there is no time more important than the rut, which is when breeding and its related activities take center stage in the deer's life. The rut is the time of greatest vulnerability for trophy bucks and the hunter's best hope for success. Because of its importance, we'll use the rut as the basis for our seasonal divisions. The divisions are the *pre-rut period*; then the two periods of the rut—the *scraping period* and the *breeding period*; and finally the *post-rut period*. These divisions represent distinct, predictable periods of whitetail activity and patterns.

The key to determining the timing of the four periods is the start of the breeding period, otherwise known as the peak of rut. The time when the major wave of does comes into estrus is well defined and seldom varies more than a day or two from year to year at any given locale. Local game departments can usually provide an accurate date for peak rut. If not, local trophy hunters can. From this one date, you can pretty well map out the four periods. This is possible because the *duration* of the two vital rut periods—the scraping and breeding periods—is fairly consistent across the country, even though when they begin isn't. With that, let's take a look at the seasonal patterns of trophy whitetails. We will only be concerned about the time of year deer are hunted. Because seasons vary so much over North America, that encompasses the entire time bucks have "hard" antlers, normally from the first of September through mid February. The accompanying graph depicts the "average" timing and length of the four periods. The following text describes how the beginning and ending points can be identified and the main characteristics of each period. We'll cover each period in greater depth later.

THE FOUR PERIODS OF FALL WHITETAIL ACTIVITY

September	October	November		December	January	February
		Scraping period	Breeding period			
PRE-RUT PERIOD				POST-RUT PERIOD		
		THE RUT				

Pre-Rut Period:

Beginning: When bucks shed the velvet from their antlers.

Key Characteristics: Predictable early morning/late afternoon feeding patterns, especially early in the period. Bachelor groups eventually break up, and mature bucks retire to their core areas. Later, feeding patterns gradually give way to increased rutting activity, i.e., more travel, scraping, checking scrapes, increased rubbing, etc. Bucks use the pre-rut to build up body fat by feeding heavily and to prepare for the approaching rut by rubbing and mock-fighting bushes and trees.

Ending: When the focus of the buck activity shifts from feeding to rutting, signaled by increased scraping and wider travel. The end of this period and the beginning of the scraping period is gradual, usually occurring over the course of a few days.

Scraping Period of the Rut:

Beginning: When bucks are more motivated by rutting than feeding activity.

Key Characteristics: Rutting activity dominates the bucks' routine and serious scrapes and rubs increase in number. Daytime movement is much greater as bucks alter and expand their range as they travel to doe group hangouts, where they make and tend scrapes. Travel patterns are now fairly predictable. This is an excellent time to hunt one particular buck on a scrapeline.

Ending: When does enter estrus and breeding begins.

Breeding Period of the Rut:

Beginning: When the first major wave of does enters estrus and breeding begins. Occurs rather suddenly and at a predictable time each year.

Key Characteristics: A marked reduction in scraping activity. Tracks of running deer are commonly seen on woods roads and along field edges. Bucks are either with a doe or looking for one. Daytime movement is at a peak. Travel patterns are unpredictable, and bucks range a great distance. Hunting a particular buck is difficult, but this is an

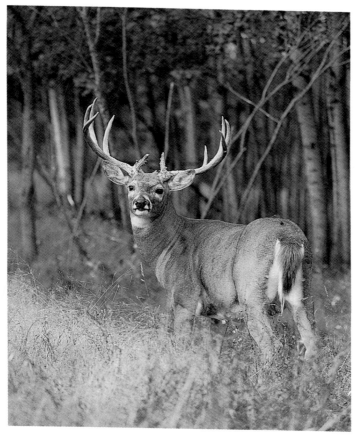

The peak rut periods are far and away the best times to hunt trophy bucks—but they aren't the only times, especially if you really under-tand whitetail movement and behavior.

excellent time to bump into preoccupied bucks rambling around with their defenses down. Most trophy bucks are killed now.

Ending: When the majority of the does have been bred and are no longer in estrus.

Post-Rut Period:

Beginning: When most does are no longer in estrus and breeding activity yields to "resting" and feeding activity.

Key Characteristics: When the frenzied peak breeding activity is over, deer movement declines noticeably. Bucks initially become reclusive and nocturnal as they recover from the rigors of the rut. Does and young bucks hold up in thickets near food sources and feed at night and during first and last light. Daylight movement is greatly reduced. After a period of rest, bucks gradually return to a feeding pattern, although they remain largely nocturnal, depending on hunting pressure. A secondary rut can initiate limited rutting activity as unbred does come into estrus a month or so after the start of the breeding period.

Ending: When the bucks drop their antlers.

CHAPTER SEVEN

THE PRE-RUT PERIOD

For both does and bucks, their summer routine revolves around food, shelter, and water. Their home range is only as large as is necessary to meet those basic needs. Throughout the summer, the bucks lead a leisurely and ordered life in bachelor groups, usually consisting of three to six bucks of similar age. Then in late summer, after their velvet-covered antlers are fully developed, a change begins in the bucks. Triggered by changes in daylength, the testicles, which have been withdrawn and functionally inactive, begin to swell and drop back into the scrotum. Testosterone, the male hormone, once again starts coursing the buck's body, bringing both physical and mental changes.

First, the bucks' antlers harden and the velvet then dries. Soon afterwards, the velvet is shed, stripped off by rubbing small trees and saplings. The shedding process is usually completed in a surprisingly short time, normally within 24 hours from start to finish. Just as significant, the bucks' shy and retiring attitude changes. They become more aggressive and restless. These changes, marked by the shedding of velvet, usher in the beginning of the pre-rut period, which occurs around the first of September over most of the country.

Now in hard antler, the bucks within the bachelor groups start showing aggression toward each other, posturing and vying for dominance as a hierarchy is established. The pre-rut is not the time of serious fighting, only occasional sparring contests to establish a pecking order. As time passes, the bucks, especially the older ones, separate and retire to their own core area, chosen largely based on security and seclusion. The core area of mature bucks is likely to be well away from the doe groups living near the prime food sources. During this time, mature bucks have little interest in does and don't intentionally interact with the doe groups, though they may feed on the same food sources. Younger bucks, however, tend to hang around the doe groups, mainly because of the nearby food sources.

After settling into their core area, most movement by mature bucks is from their bedding area to feeding grounds and back again. Generally, activity is limited during this time and they feed near their core area. If they have to travel to find adequate food, they do so early and late in the day or at night. Mature bucks tend to be nocturnal during this time and can be very hard to hunt. Factors such as hunting pressure, herd density, weather, terrain, cover and the distribution of food sources all figure into how hard a pre-rut buck will be to line up in a set of sights. Although a buck does not necessarily feed in the same place or travel the same trails every day, his travel pattern is repetitive and somewhat predictable. However, changes can occur rather abruptly if a food source peters out or a better source becomes available.

As bucks travel to and from feeding and bedding areas, they hone their fighting skills on bushes and small trees and do some "pawing," leaving rubs and preliminary scrapes along the trails and in the areas where they spend the most time. Rubbing and mock fights with bushes build their testosterone-rich muscles and help them get the "feel" of their new antlers. This is all part of their preparation for the coming rut and will bring progressive physical changes culminating in a masculine, big-necked animal ready to compete for breeding rights. The catalyst is ever-increasing amounts of testosterone, which has the same effect as steroids on an athlete in training.

As the end of the pre-rut period approaches, bucks start to rub with more aggression, sometimes shredding bushes and small trees. Threats and posturing—hackles up and ears back—often accompany buck encounters. The previously haphazard pawings now more resemble serious scrapes. Bucks begin to show interest in does. The feeding pattern becomes less predictable as the bucks shift their focus from food to females. Their travel distance and time increase as they begin making long forays checking doe groups and revisiting their traditional scraping areas, laying down more serious sign as they go. With that, the pre-rut has ended and the rut has begun.

KEY ELEMENTS OF THE PRE-RUT

Sign:
Rubs, trails, tracks, scrapes (more like pawings) and droppings are all helpful sign during the pre-rut. But short of having seen the buck, which is by far my first choice, rubs most dependably identify the presence of a big buck. While not 100 percent reliable, the general rule is that bigger bucks make bigger rubs. More accurately, large, medium and small bucks can make small or medium-sized rubs, but big rubs are almost always made by big (at least big-bodied) bucks. I have seen small bucks rub large, well-worn trees, but I feel certain these small bucks were not responsible for making the rubs originally. They were just contributing their "mark" to an already established rub.

Rubs, unlike true scrapes, don't necessarily promise a

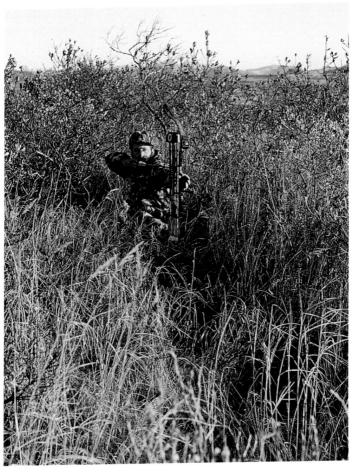

Suitable tactics for pre-rut hunting depend to some extent on the equipment chosen. Rubs and feeding patterns are key elements, but the bowhunter has to adjust his plan for close-range work.

buck's imminent return. The exception might be what is known as a "signpost rub," which is a particularly well-worn rub that dominant bucks, and other bucks as well, seem to use repeatedly as a sight and scent-marker, much like a true breeding scrape is used. Of course, an abundance of rubs in one location does indicate a buck has spent time there and may do so again. For this reason, I'm more interested in rublines consisting of several large, fresh rubs than in a single rub.

The actual size of a "large" rub varies by location across the continent. The key is to look for something big for that area. In Canada and Montana, I've seen rubs on fenceposts and road-sign posts, as well as on eight to 10-inch trees. Big-bodied, northern bucks rub impressive trees, commonly two to four inches in diameter. In southern regions, rubs tend to be smaller, mainly because the deer are smaller. Rub trees in the 1½ to three-inch range would be targets for big bucks there. In addition to tree size, the depth of the tine gouges, the amount of broken and twisted limbs, the length and height of the rub and the overall degree of damage are also clues to a buck's size.

Half-hearted pawings, called "boundary" or "trail" scrapes, are another useful pre-rut sign. They are not as large or as well-defined as the clean, yard-long "breeding scrapes" to come later. These pre-rut scrapes are probably made instinctively as a foreshadowing of future serious scraping activity. Or perhaps, like rubs, they are visual and scent-markers serving notice of a buck's presence. Whatever their purpose, they are not necessarily an indicator that the buck will return to that place unless their number alone points to high usage. Their location and their abundance, however, can be important pieces of the patterning puzzle.

A brief word on tracks. Big tracks usually indicate good body size, and big bodies often have big racks setting atop them. But, that is far from foolproof. What's on a buck's head sometimes bears little relevance to foot size. Still, I'll take big tracks over little ones any day.

Feeding Areas:

Feeding areas are the best starting points for patterning pre-rut bucks. Fortunately, they often are easy to find and identify. The ideal setup is when there are only a few distinct food sources to choose from. A good example would be when several square miles of woodlands adjoin a handful of fields planted in desirable agricultural crops, such as corn, soybeans, winter wheat, oats, alfalfa, etc. Deer would feed heavily on these crops. The worst situation is an expansive tract of uniform timber without any concentrated food sources. In such cases, deer will disperse throughout their range to feed, making them hard to pattern.

It is also possible to have too much of a good thing. Areas with many choices of preferred foods, such as farmlands of the Midwest and Central Canada, can make predicting travel patterns difficult. A widely distributed acorn crop also can cause this. Still, food sources remain the best beginning point for finding pre-rut bucks.

Now comes a problem—mature bucks often avoid exposed major food sources used by does, fawns and young bucks, at least during daylight hours. Instead of exposing themselves in the open or "eating out" with the crowd, trophy bucks typically opt to feed at secondary food sources, usually ones close to their bedding area or ones with some protective cover like a clearcut. Or, they may indeed feed at the most popular hangouts with other deer . . . but at night. Many hunters waste precious time watching food sources filled with does and fawns while mature bucks feed at out-of-the-way secondary sources or sleep the day away. Hunting pressure will virtually always cause this, but it is often the case even when pressure is light.

As the pre-rut period progresses, levels of testosterone increase, creating dramatic changes in a buck's habits and personality.

Once you've located a feeding area, there are some key places to look for big rubs. First, rubs may be found in or around the feeding area. In the case of agricultural fields, rubs are frequently made along the edges. When deer are feeding on acorns or in other areas of cover, rubs may be seen in the feeding area itself.

Second, deer commonly stage (hole up) some 100 to 200 yards inside cover (usually on the downwind side of the food source from the prevailing wind) before entering a field or an exposed food source just before or after dark. To identify these staging areas, look for signs of heavy deer use such as droppings, tracks, browse sign and trails, particularly intersecting trails and trails running parallel to the food source. Bucks often make rubs and preliminary scrapes in these staging grounds.

The third place is along the connecting trails. As bucks

amble along trails, they frequently make rubs. They seem to have a particular affinity for rub-making where trails parallel streambottoms. Rubs along trails are invaluable in revealing where the buck is coming from and going to. They also allow a hunter to distinguish between the trails of does, fawns and young bucks and those of mature bucks. Ideally, buck trails would have enough rubs along them to allow a hunter to backtrack to bedding and/or feeding areas. While the story occasionally does unravel that cleanly, some extrapolation is usually called for.

One last place rubs can be found in numbers is in and around bedding areas. Bucks often loiter around their bedding site when not lying down and will make rubs while doing so. An abundance of rubs in a likely bedding area may be the tipoff you're in a buck's bedroom. Since bedding areas are more secluded, they are the least likely place to find rubs, at least in the early going.

Bedding Sites:
Figuring out where a buck beds is an important part of patterning him. Unfortunately, this is not always easy. Such things as the terrain, cover, the distance the buck is traveling, the amount of sign and your access to all the buck's range factor into what you're up against. In reality, you usually know only part of the travel pattern of the buck you're hunting. As we saw in our discussion of rubs, they can be a help in pointing the way to bedding sites. And happily, trophy buck bedding areas share certain characteristics that allow us to make educated guesses about where they might be if we can't definitively pin them down. During most of the pre-rut, a mature buck's bedding site is in his core area, the fairly small acreage where he spends most of his time. It's a fair bet the cover will be thick and the bedding place secluded. Mature bucks do not like to be

disturbed in their beds. Bedding sites usually offer either some downwind visibility or are located in ground cover, such as dense underbrush, blowdowns, low-growing evergreens, tall grass, cattails, cane, etc., thick enough that a threat cannot approach without being heard well in advance. Bucks seem to like to bed near beaver ponds, sloughs, and other such places with standing water, probably because of the dense cover often found there and the partial protection and escape route the water side affords. Bucks bed where they have a choice of escape routes to avoid getting hemmed in or cornered. Also, good access to feeding areas and water is a preference.

In hot weather, bucks will bed where they have both shade and a breeze (if they can find one), which usually means a sidehill if the terrain allows. In cold weather, they seek out sunny sites to warm themselves, which means a southern exposure in rolling terrain.

In hilly country, bucks seem to choose elevated places to bed, most commonly on the side of hills rather than right on top. If possible, they will bed facing downhill and downwind in a place that gives them a decent view. This allows the bucks to use their incredible sense of smell to detect danger coming from their uphill blindside. Anything approaching from below and downwind will be seen.

Flatland bucks often employ a similar strategy to that of bucks in hilly terrain when choosing where in a piece of cover they'll bed. As in hilly areas, they use the wind to protect their blindside behind them and try to bed where they can see some distance downwind. I've seen this often in the small woodlots in Canada where the snow tells the story clearly. There, bucks tend to bed on the downwind side of woodlots where they can smell danger approaching through the dense timber and where they can see downwind into the open fields. Bucks bedding in thick cover inside an area of thinner cover employ this same scheme.

Connecting Trails:

Obviously, the trails connecting bedding areas to feeding areas are important to hunters. As we've said, you'll be lucky indeed if you can backtrack along trails and reconstruct a buck's travel pattern. The trails are normally too indistinct to follow all the way. Conversely, there may be a profusion of intersecting trails and overall deer sign that is too confusing to help pattern any particular buck. Snow would help but is seldom present during the pre-rut. Usually, you can follow trails far enough to at least speculate on what the buck is doing.

Food sources are a good place to start the search for trails. The number and complexity of trails will depend on the importance of the food source and the herd density. I begin by looking for a concentration of tracks. In open food sources like agricultural fields, deer usually have preferred entry points, such as corners of the field, behind islands of cover and secluded parts of the field. These entry points will be heavily tracked, and trails will be nearby. In a major feeding area, does, fawns, and young bucks are sure to be feeding there and will create an elaborate network of trails. Check for big rubs and other evidence that a good buck is using the trails. Also, don't limit your search to the major entry points; trophy bucks sometimes enter a feeding area well away from the crowds.

Once trails into a feeding area are located, try to backtrack them to the staging areas inside the cover. Do this whether or not you've found big rubs on the trails entering the food source. Staging areas, which are not always easy to find and identify, are excellent places to hunt night-feeding bucks since they may arrive there before dark. The presence of big rubs will tell you if a staging area holds promise.

When you've found a trail with promising rubs, follow it out to learn as much as possible about what the buck is doing. Determine whether the trail is a "going-to-feed" trail used in the afternoon or a "back-to-bed" trail used in the morning, or both. The rubs themselves will help you decide this. If all the rubs along a trail are on the same side of trees and bushes, you can assume the buck is traveling in only one direction on that trail, from the side with the rubs. If rubs are on both sides, the buck is using the same trail coming and going, assuming it's the same buck. In places with high deer populations, it's hard to sort out one particular buck from all the sign, but big rubs will tell you that at least one good buck has been there.

As trails lead farther from feeding areas, they become fainter and harder to read. By the time they reach a buck's core area, they will have fingered out and pretty much dissipated. However, rubs may be present along the faint trails near a bedding area and are almost certain to be found in the bedding area itself. Be careful as you near a bedding area. If disturbed much there, mature bucks will hit the high road ... for good.

Doe Groups:

Doe groups or "family units", as they are often called because they usually consist of related deer, are made up of from two to 20 or more does and fawns. Young bucks often hang out with them, mainly because good chow is inevitably nearby. The doe groups are led by a matriarch or "alpha" doe. In low density herds, doe groups are distinct and spend much of their time apart from other groups. In high populations, they are far less distinctive and more intermingled, sometimes to the point that it is impossible to tell that a doe-group structure exists at all.

Doe groups occupy the best habitat in an area, and their home range is closely associated with prime food sources. Mature bucks don't have much to do with the doe groups most of the year, but they know where the doe groups are in their neck of the woods. When the rut arrives, they hot-foot it to them.

HUNTING THE PRE-RUT

The pre-rut period offers no better than a fair chance for a trophy. Top-end bucks are downright tough then, even under favorable circumstances. If the deer are pressured to any degree, mature bucks become mostly nocturnal and difficult to pattern. Still, if the hunter does his homework, there is opportunity in the pre-rut.

Pre-rut hunting should start with topographic maps and aerial photographs of the area to be hunted. These tools will allow you to quickly identify potential feeding and bedding areas, travel routes, bottlenecks, ambush points, etc. They will save you considerable time and effort and provide "access" to land you don't have permission to go on. Using them, you can postulate a theory about what a buck is doing over his entire range and then make efficient use of the leg work required to prove out your theory.

One of the first pieces of the puzzle I want to know is the level of hunting pressure. Feeding deer are highly sensitive to pressure, and this goes in spades for mature bucks. Next, I want to scout out the major and secondary food sources. I check overall deer sign and look for general movement patterns, but ultimately, my goal is to find big buck sign, namely big rubs. I'm particularly interested in the more secluded food sources in or near thick cover even if they are inferior in scope or quality to the more accessible, open sources.

Once I find big rubs, I try to learn as much as I can without overly disturbing the place. I identify the trails and backtrack them, trying to figure out where they lead and who's using them. I seek out the staging area and try to understand the story the tracks, droppings, trails, and rubs in and around it tell. Based on the hunting pressure, the time of the year and the deer sign present, I develop a strategy.

Let's address how hunting pressure figures in first. As a rule-of-thumb, the lighter the pressure, the nearer the actual food source you can hunt. Conversely, the heavier the pressure, the closer to the bedding area you must hunt. All things being equal, when pressure is very light (practically nonexistent), my preference is to hunt the food source itself. As the destination point, this is the most dependable place to wait out a buck. If there is any pressure at all, I'll abandon the food source per se in favor of the staging area, which is really my first choice for trophy bucks anyway. The only reason I opt first for the food source when there is no pressure is because the likelihood of being picked off by lesser deer in the tight quarters of a staging area is greater than in the normally "roomer" feeding area. If the area has moderate hunting pressure, I move farther from the food source to trails with big rubs, hoping to find bottlenecks, powerlines, or other intercept points along travel routes from bedding to feeding areas. Finally, if pressure is heavy, I set up as near to the bedding area as possible or on the farthermost trail with good sign.

The time of year has much to do with the strategy. The best time to catch a buck on a food source, especially an open one, during daylight hours is within the first two weeks after shedding their velvet. During this time, the bucks are on the tail-end of their predictable, summer feeding pattern. Afterwards, the daytime feeding pattern begins to breakdown as the bucks spend more and more time in their core area and become increasingly nocturnal. Staging areas and travel lanes are now the places of choice. Toward the end of the period, as their interest in does increases, the bucks start traveling more and spending more time around the doe groups, which are sure to be near food sources. This increased travel expands your choices of ambush points.

Stand-hunting is generally the best plan during the pre-rut. About the only still-hunting (slipping around) I will do during this time is while hunting/scouting prospective new places. Even then, I spend a lot of time sitting and leaning against trees, especially during prime hours and when I'm in a good location. Bucks tend to be cautious and careful during the pre-rut. It's not easy to slip up on them.

Deer drives can be a good alternative tactic during the pre-rut, especially during warm spells when deer movement is low. Known bedding areas are good places to push during midday hours. Early morning drives near feeding areas can be productive if you can get set up without spooking all the bucks from the area. The main drawback to drives is that they disrupt natural movement, an important consideration when limited to a small tract or hunting one particular buck.

Rattling during the beginning and middle of the pre-rut period is spotty at best. Passive rattling works best then, if it works at all. Just tickle the antlers together very gingerly a few times and wait. Actually, mild brush-rubbing might work as well as rattling. Naturally, rattling response picks up at an accelerating rate as the bucks' interest starts to shift from food to does toward the end of the pre-rut period.

CHAPTER EIGHT

THE SCRAPING PERIOD OF THE RUT

"Good. More buck sign here now than when I put the stand up two days ago," I thought as I scanned the area with my binoculars from the treestand. "At least two fresh rubs over there, and the ground is really torn up along the edge of those spruces. That wasn't there before. It's just starting. I ought to be hitting it just right."

I had found the area a year earlier during the middle of Saskatchewan's rut. The place was wrecked. Poplar and spruce trees nearly as thick as my thigh had their bark shredded through to bare wood. Scars from rubs made in years past marred tree trunks in every direction. Several car-door sized scrapes were churned clean of forest litter, the debris thrown 20 feet away. The musky scent of rutting bucks permeated the air. The joint bordered on spooky.

For three days last year, I sat on the spot—and saw several decent bucks. but I knew I was too late for the main action. In all likelihood, the dominant bucks had already broken off their normal travel patterns and gotten with a hot doe. Sure, a whopper buck could have walked into such a traditional scraping area as this any time, but I had missed the time of greatest opportunity. I filed that place away in my mind. Next year I would be there when the bucks first started making the sign. Then, I would have my best chance of seeing what was there.

Now, the many old scars on the trees reminded me just how hot this little semi-clearing in the deep forest could be. I had four days left for the right buck to show up and for the scraping period of the rut to heat up. As I was about to find out, it wouldn't take that long.

Noon was approaching. The cold had pretty well seeped to my bones, and I was stiff from hours of motionless sitting in the cramped stand. Besides, rental time on the three cups of coffee that had jump-started me before dawn had run out. I needed to get down and move around. But first, I would try another rattling sequence. I had already rattled in a 140-class, 10-pointer earlier that morning. And the two other smaller bucks that had come in later had checked the scrapes and made new rubs. The timing was right for rattling.

I positioned my gun for quick access and began the sequence by gently tickling the tines of the horns together. Gradually, I picked up the tempo until I was twisting and turning the antlers together smartly. I was no more than a minute into the process when I saw him coming at a fast trot. I immediately traded the horns for my 7mm Remington Magnum. The buck abruptly halted about 60 yards away, his head and neck nearly completely obscured by two trees. I grabbed for my 10-power Leicas to try to figure out exactly what he was wearing upstairs. Through my glasses, I could see the buck was huge in the body and that he was desperately looking for the source of the ruckus. Then, a dark, heavy antler briefly swung clear of the obscuring trees, revealing a heavy beam with four good primary tines standing! A 12-pointer . . . if he had brows and the other side matched. He gave me no time to find out.

The buck whirled around, trotted away a few yards and came to a tentative halt, his head and most of his body blocked my trees and bushes. Only about a half-foot of the base of his massive neck was clearly visible through my scope. Time to shoot or forget it. I would have to chance it on the basis of what I'd seen. The buck fell where he stood when the 140-grain Nosler Partition struck him.

When I walked up to him, I couldn't believe the enormity of the animal. He was easily the largest-bodied whitetail I had ever seen. After gawking at the 400-pound-plus buck, I finally got around to checking his antlers. The one side, as I had seen, sported six points; the other side five. On the strength of 11 long tines and good mass, his score edged into the 160s. Such is the opportunity offered during the scraping period of the rut.

TIMING AND DURATION

The scraping period more or less "emerges" from the end of the pre-rut period. Increasing levels of testosterone doing its work, the bucks become more restless, aggressive and preoccupied by their sexual desire with each passing day. Finally, when the bucks shift their priority from food and security to the urge to reproduce, the scraping period is underway.

At any given location, the scraping period occurs at a predictable time each year, as would be expected with any day/length controlled function. The length of the period is quite consistent across the country. However, exactly when the scraping period begins varies greatly from one location to another since its timing is directly related to when breeding occurs, which can be as early as September in some locations and as late as January in others. Fortunately, if we know the length of the scraping period and when the breeding period starts, we can accurately forecast the timing of the scraping period. Let's start with the duration.

Although significant scraping activity can sometimes be seen three or more weeks before the start of breeding, my experiences lead me to believe that the scraping period lasts about two weeks in most places. Serious, consistent scraping, the trademark of this period, simply cannot be counted on much earlier than two weeks prior to the start of breeding. And actually, the main event, i.e., the making of serious breeding scrapes and rubs (I'll describe these a little later), doesn't usually crank up until about seven to 10 days before breeding starts.

So, if the scraping period lasts two weeks, then when it starts can be determined by backing up two weeks from the beginning date for peak breeding, which local game biologists or serious trophy hunters can tell you. For example, a November 15 start-up date for peak breeding means that the scraping period would begin around November 1 with the intensity of activity and sign-making really picking up between November 4 and 7.

KEY SIGN: BREEDING SCRAPES AND RUBS

Scrapes perform a very specific and unique role in the whitetail breeding ritual. The serious scrapes made by bucks during the onset of the rut are called "breeding scrapes", and it would behoove every trophy hunter to know as much as possible about them.

Breeding scrapes are large, well-defined, oval-shaped areas of ground pawed completely clean of leaves and debris. They may range in size from two to five feet in diameter. About four to 4½ feet above the scrape, there virtually always will be an overhanging limb that has been mangled

The author rattled in this 28-inch 10-pointer near the end of the scraping period, the time when rattling generally works best.

and broken, the aftermath of the buck's sometimes violent attempt to leave his scent on the limb from his forehead or preorbital glands, or even his saliva as he frequently will bite the small branches and pull them through his mouth. The ground in a fresh scrape will be "plowed up", damp and often musky smelling. This odor is because both bucks and does urinate over their tarsal glands (located on their hind legs) onto the scrape, leaving their "calling card" for a would-be mate. Often, there will be a string of scrapes together called a scrapeline.

Breeding rubs are usually in association with breeding scrapes. Hormones running high, bucks work themselves into a lather when engaged in the serious work of setting the bait for a hot doe. At some point, they release their pent-up frustration on nearby bushes and trees, often shedding or maybe even breaking in two their chosen target. Like scrapes, several rubs are usually together, making up a rubline. Breeding rubs together with breeding scrapes serve as scent and sight-markers that signify a buck's presence, breeding readiness, and quite likely his relative status on the dominance ladder.

While scrapes are created and maintained primarily by bucks, does also check and use scrapes to see who's in the market for action and to signal their own readiness to breed as estrus approaches. Like the bucks, does will actually paw the ground and urinate over their tarsal glands in scrapes as a form of scent communication. It is even believed that the dominant doe in an area will intentionally seek out the dominant buck in order to breed with him. When does come to scrapes, they tend to spend more time in the vicinity than do bucks. After all, does normally live in the area. Mature bucks, on the other hand, probably don't. Plus, they are usually in a hurry to check out some other place.

More than one buck will use a scrape. I'm not yet convinced it is common practice for more than one *dominant* buck to use the same scrape, but I do know that small bucks will check and "touch up" the scrape of a larger buck. An active scrapeline in a soon-to-be-hot area is a focal point of deer interest and activity. It's only logical that young or subdominant bucks keep an eye on the local "pickup corner" when Mr. Big is away.

Breeding rubs and scrapes are often found at the staging grounds near major food sources, if any are present, but are practically always found along an edge of some type. Seldom-used logging roads, the edges of clearings and fields, old homesites, the break between two timber types and along stream and lake edges are favored places for scrapes and rubs. One of the very best places to check is where you've seen them in years past. Barring changes in the habitat, these "traditional scraping areas," are "social hubs" where mature bucks return each year to make breeding scrapes and rubs. They will be used year after year, even if the buck, or one of the bucks, making the sign was shot there. The attraction of that area is not limited to just one buck, and another buck will take the place of the one removed.

How can you tell what size buck is using a scrape? The size of the scrape, the damage to the overhanging limb and the general disturbance of the area surrounding the scrape are good indicators. An excellent clue to the magnitude of the buck is the size of the rubs associated with scrapes.

BUCK PATTERNS DURING THE PERIOD

Bucks start out the scraping period using their core area as their base of operations. Instead of traveling mostly to and from their feeding grounds as they did during the pre-rut, their destination is now doe groups, some of which may be a mile, two miles, or even more from their core area. Bucks make scouting passes through the home ranges of doe groups, locating the high-activity areas and checking out the territory, especially the traditional scraping areas. On these early runs, the bucks make preliminary "test" scrapes and rubs, especially in the traditional scraping areas, and may even feed a bit on nearby major food sources.

A few days into the scraping period, the bucks start their work in earnest. Their route and routine now pretty well established, the bucks begin making serious breeding scrapes. Now, the pace of the deer world really picks up. The mature bucks begin a somewhat predictable routine of making, checking, and maintaining scrapes at the social hubs of the various doe groups. The younger bucks randomly work the doe groups and make half-baked scrapes, usually near the major feeding areas, and check the scrapes of the mature bucks, hoping to get in on whatever action may occur. Does continue to feed, but their schedule becomes more and more disrupted by their own restlessness and by the evermore persistent bucks.

In addition to working their scrapes, bucks begin seeking out does in hopes of catching their first whiff of the coming estrus. The does, their tails tucked, their bodies hunched while keeping low to the ground, scurry away from their impassioned suitors. Should the doe urinate, the buck excitedly sniffs and licks the discharge, sometimes raising his head high and curling his upper lip. This is called "flehmening", and according to researchers, what the buck is actually doing is using his tongue to place the scent on the roof of his mouth so it can be "smelled" by a small structure there called the Jacobson's organ. The apparent purpose is to help get the buck's breeding readiness on the same schedule as that of the does in his area.

Growing aggression during the scraping period leads to challenges and fights between bucks of similar size. Mature bucks are now ranging well beyond their familiar territory where a hierarchy has been established among area bucks. During their travels, they encounter other mature bucks that offer challenge. Threats and posturing ensue, and when that doesn't settle the matter, fights break out. Some can be serious, but the most violent fights come during the breeding period, when a hot doe is the direct prize.

Within a few days of the beginning of widespread scraping, another change begins. The promising scent of soon-to-be-ready does is in the air, perhaps first picked up by the bucks at their scrapes. This alluring scent disrupts the bucks' travel routine and rewrites their schedule. They start to spend less time working their scrapes and more time actually checking out does. Their travels become less predictable. The bucks spend more time near the doe groups, even bedding near them, returning to their core area less frequently. They travel feverishly from one doe group to another, seeking the receptive doe they know will soon appear . . . or perhaps hoping to find and claim one of the early starters. The maddening scent of approaching estrus filling the woods, they eagerly check each doe they encounter. And then, it happens.

Finally, the unmistakable scent of a hot doe fills a big buck's nostrils, perhaps rising from one of his scrapes. The buck searches frantically for the departing trail. Moments later, he hits it and weaves back and forth along the trail for 10 yards before locking onto the alluring scent with un-wavering certainty. Intent on one thing, he goes off in a short-gaited trot. Unerringly, his nose takes him to the doe. She is ready but teasingly unwilling to receive his advances. A chase follows. This same scene is played out across the land. The first major wave of does has entered estrus, the scraping period has ended and the breeding festivities have begun.

With this profile of the scraping period, you probably see why this time of year offers hunters their best opportunity to successfully hunt one particular buck. On a fairly predictable travel pattern while working their scrapes and distracted by the lure of the rut, trophy bucks that seldom expose themselves to danger in daylight hours are now more vulnerable. This is a time trophy hunters do not want to miss.

HUNTING STRATEGY

Scrape hunting, more than any other type of hunting, is truly a matter of being in the right place at the right time.

The right place is where a big buck is making or checking breeding scrapes and rubs; the right time is when he first starts making and checking the sign. It is the critical timing that presents a special problem for the hunter. You see, by the time widespread sign is present in the woods, the most productive time to hunt that sign may well be past. When bucks first start making and checking breeding scrapes and rubs, that is their most pressing priority at the moment and their activity patterns are somewhat predictable. But in a matter of only a few days (I feel that magic window is only five days or so), their priority begins to shift from setting a bait for does to the does themselves. With that, bucks begin to spend less time at their scrapes and more time on the move after prospective does, reducing the odds of catching them on their scrapes.

So, we have a dilemma. By the time we find an active scrapeline, the best time to hunt it could have passed. What's the answer? You could scout everyday for the first evidence of a soon-to-be-active scrapeline, but that eats into valuable hunting time and you might be looking for something that doesn't even exist yet. Plus, the time spent looking could be the very time you should have been on the stand watching the scraping area. Or, you could take the time-honored approach and scout after the sign is made, but you may find yourself watching where a buck has been rather than where he will be! A better way is to hunt traditional scraping areas.

Traditional scraping areas are places where rut-struck bucks go year after year to advertise their presence and readiness to breed to local doe groups by making breeding scrapes and rubs. Contrary to popular belief, more than one buck uses such an area, although one may be dominant and the chief sign-maker. Both the local doe groups and the bucks hoping to connect with a hot doe from those

Guy Shanks of Bigfork, Montana, shot this heavy buck in a traditional scraping area just as the bucks were starting to make scrapes.

groups are well aware of such areas long before the rut cranks up and the first serious rutting sign is laid down. True, scrapes and rubs will be made in places other than traditional scraping areas, but the other places don't offer the same advantage of predictability or similar odds that the dominant buck in those parts will show up there.

One big plus for traditional scraping areas is that scouting for them can be done during the off-season. In regions with little or no snow, immediately after the season closes is the ideal time. In snow country, the time of choice is just after snowmelt. The earlier you go, the better the chances the scrapes will still be evident and the rubs will still be shining.

How do you find and recognize traditional scraping areas? Let's start with a reminder. In heavily hunted herds with mostly young bucks, the normal behavioral patterns are disrupted and competition is reduced. Because of this, the traditional scraping areas are either so indistinguishable as to be hard to find or absent altogether. In such cases, hunters generally have to hunt whatever decent buck sign they can find and hope for the best.

Where pressure is light to moderate, traditional scraping areas will be present. You just have to find them. If major food sources are present, the search should start there. Look for breaks and edges of some type close to the food source or in the nearby staging area. Small openings, logging roads, breaks in cover or timber types, and especially stream edges are all prime sites for traditional scraping areas.

When you find a traditional scraping area, it won't be hard to recognize it. There will be lots of sign, most notably rubs and scrapes, but the one thing that will verify the identity of a traditional scraping area is the presence of rubs of varying ages. There will probably be rubs on top of older rubs. Scrapes obviously don't have the longevity of rubs, but even after evidence of scrapes has been erased from the ground, the telltale mangled limbs above them will still reveal their presence.

A traditional scraping area invariably has trails leading to and from it. The area is, after all, a social hub for deer during the fall. Study the area and try to figure out the overall travel pattern. Now's the time to decide on a stand site and perhaps even to hang a stand. Walk the trails out, learn the terrain, determine the predominant wind direction in the fall, choose an approach route and clear a shooting lane if necessary. Write down what you've seen and decided. Have everything ready so you just walk in and hunt next fall . . . just as the sign is first being made!

Stand-hunting is generally the best way to hunt scrapes. I prefer portable stands over permanent ones. The portable should be one that can be hung quickly and quietly. A ground stand is also fine, but you are more likely to be seen or smelled on the ground than if you're up a tree.

It is critical that the area not be disturbed. Bucks depend heavily on their noses now, and your scent won't go undetected if spread around. The use of cover scent may be helpful. Rubber-bottomed boots will help since they don't pick up and transfer odor like other boots. Try not to let your clothes or body rub against vegetation near the scrapeline or approach route. Depending on the setup, I am of the general opinion that your odds decrease the longer you hunt a particular stand, especially in tight quarters where the deer are sure to eventually pick you out. For this reason, I try to choose the very best time to hunt a promising scraping area.

Rattling and grunting can be very effective when hunting scrapes. But when on stand, calling must be done sparingly and, in the case of rattling, rather passively, especially during the prime movement hours. Rattling or grunting repeatedly from a stationary position always has the potential of drawing attention to yourself and is particularly dicey when you're in a tight, high-activity area. For this reason, when I suspect deer are on the move in the vicinity, I rattle or call only enough to entice them into the area but hopefully not enough to give them an exact fix on my location. During midday hours or later in the scraping period when bucks are spending more time looking for does than checking scrapes, I will call or rattle with more frequency and vigor.

Bucks can approach scrapes from anywhere, regardless of the wind direction, but the tendency is to come in from downwind or crosswind. Even when they approach from crosswind, they'll usually end up downwind, especially if they are winding the scrape rather than actually working it. Because of this, it is best to locate your stand well downwind of scrapes, or better yet, downwind but to the opposite side of the buck's suspected approach route. I like to be as

Steve Spears and the author teamed up to rattle in this 23-inch eight-pointer during the scraping period. The author shot this buck in full stride at eight yards.

far away from the scrapes as reasonable to reduce the likelihood that other deer investigating the area will give me away to the buck I'm after.

In the event you can't find a specific place to pin your hopes on during the scraping period, slipping slowly and quietly through areas with buck sign or around food sources can also be good. It allows you to scout even while hunting. I've killed many good bucks this way. The increased buck activity alone greatly improves the odds of coming across a preoccupied buck. If you prefer to stand-hunt, try to find cutlines, bottlenecks and other advantageous stand sites close to the best buck sign available or on the way to food sources. Unless the pressure is high, which means nocturnal activity, or time is running out, I don't like to drive deer during the scraping time. This can disrupt their natural movement patterns.

The scraping period, especially the latter part, is the best time for antler rattling. Bucks are "wired" and full of themselves. When they hear the sound of a "buck fight," their aggression takes over and they come looking for action. You don't have to be bashful about rattling now. I do start off slowly so I don't startle nearby deer. But by the time the sequence is over, the rattling horns—and usually my knuckles— have taken a pretty good beating. I like to add realism to the process by rubbing trees, breaking limbs and stomping the ground. I often spend all day this time of year moving from place to place and rattling. When the bucks are turned on, rattling has to be one of the most exciting forms of hunting.

CHAPTER NINE

THE BREEDING PERIOD OF THE RUT

I've got a little dog named Gizmo. He's a Shih Tzu, a breed I'd never heard of until my daughters brought one home for keeps six years ago. Gizmo might weigh eight pounds. My nephew, Trey, has a chocolate lab named Abby. She's a whopper, easily topping 70 pounds. Trey and Abby live a quarter-mile from me. A while back, Abby came into heat . . . and life in my house became darn-near unbearable.

You see, when Abby's alluring aroma first wafted over our way, Gizmo, normally a calm, happy-go-lucky pooch, transformed into a single-minded, sex-crazed canine pest. He began scratching on doors, barking without apparent cause and performing obscene gestures on any leg that remained stationary for more than 10 seconds. When he did gain access to the outside, he would set sail to Abby's house as fast as his five-inch legs would take him, though I can't imagine what good it would have done him to have caught up with his would-be Amazon girlfriend.

To make matters worse, Trey brought Abby over to my house a couple of times while in her enticing condition, driving Gizmo—and therefore me—completely bonkers. And, after wetting the yard in several places, Abby effectively left her calling card at my very back door to further incite riot in Gizmo . . . and to attract a steady stream of amorous male dogs that came from only God knows

Running deer tracks in fresh snow led the author to a breeding party that included this 155-class Montana buck.

where. The whole affair was a big aggravation, but it did once again show me the irresistible power of the breeding urge. And you know what? It's no different in deer.

Just as Gizmo took leave of his senses in the presence of a hot female, so it is with bucks during the rut. When the long-awaited breeding time finally rolls around, which it does only once a year (that in itself helps explain its fierce intensity), the normally cautious, retiring whitetail buck becomes a bold, nomadic bundle of male hormones. With the urge to breed vying with survival as the top priority in their lives, the rut is the only time mature bucks lower their rather formidable defenses and expose themselves during daylight hours with any consistency. The siren-scent of a ready doe is so powerful that it can lure even a mature buck into places no self-respecting whitetail would ever dare venture outside the rut. An encounter I had during a hunt in Canada a couple of years ago will illustrate the point.

I was driving to lunch through a snow-covered, treeless stretch of farm country when a dark clump up ahead gradually transformed into a high 160s 11-pointer trying to flatten himself out in the ditch alongside the road. His lady friend lay nonchalantly at his side. The nearest cover was but a faint streak on the distant horizon. Unfortunately for me, I had just left the legal hunting zone for nonresidents. Unfortunately for the deer, the pickup behind me contained two residents.

Such a thing would happen only under the blinding influence of the sexual urge. Random movement like this may make hunting a particular buck difficult, but no matter . . . random though it may be, there is simply no better time to cross paths with a trophy whitetail than during the breeding period.

Breeding Period Basics:

First, let's explore some basics about the breeding period. The rut comes on rather suddenly when the first wave of does enters estrus. True, a few does come into heat earlier and some later than the majority, but it's the first big wave, made up primarily of does 2½ years old and older, that brings on the frenzied breeding activity known as the "peak of rut." This critical time, which lasts about two weeks, is what we define as the breeding period. All things being equal, the heaviest breeding activity actually takes place during the first seven to 10 days and then tails off after that.

About 26 to 28 days after the peak period, a smaller second group of does, consisting mostly of 1½-year-olds but also including any older doe that didn't conceive during the first go-around, will enter estrus and trigger the "secondary rut." This occurs during what we've designated as the post-rut period. Additionally, 26 to 28 days after the secondary rut a minor "tertiary rut" occurs when six-month-old fawns enter estrus for the first time, which will include from 20 to 50 percent of the fawns in a healthy herd. As far as the hunter is concerned, both the secondary and tertiary ruts are of far less importance than the peak breeding period.

The timing of the breeding period varies greatly throughout the whitetail's range. Certainly, November is the main month for breeding across the country, but it can be as early as August, as is the case in South Florida, or as late as January, as is so in Alabama. The timing of peak rut is determined by nature based on when the fawns have the best chance to survive. Harsh environmental conditions, such as floods, cold, drought, etc., can create a relatively narrow window for maximum fawn survival. Local game departments and experienced hunters can tell you when peak breeding occurs where you hunt.

The whitetail rutting scheme assures keen competition between bucks. The reason is that all the bucks are ready to breed but only a certain percentage of the does are in heat at any given time even during the peak of breeding. To illustrate, let's assume that the breeding period lasts 14 days and that 70 percent of the does are bred during this time. That would mean an average of only five percent of the does, which are each in estrus for only 24 hours, would be receptive on any given day. In actuality, the peak activity is skewed toward the beginning of the period, thus some early days will see a higher percentage of does in estrus, perhaps as high as 10 to 15 percent. The spreading out of does entering estrus even within the peak breeding period is a built-in mechanism to give dominant bucks every chance to do most of the breeding, assuring competition in most herds.

Under high pressure, as we've discussed, the buck/doe ratio and the buck age structure can get so badly out of whack that the available mature bucks simply can't get to all the does. When this happens, young or inferior bucks participate in breeding at an unnatural level and competition among mature bucks is reduced.

The Pattern of the Period:

In the gray light of first dawn, the buck alternately trots and walks down the familiar trail that will take him to his scrapes in the small clearing near the edge of the cornfield. In a stiff-legged trot, he covers the last 50 yards to the wash-tub sized scrape. Even before he noses the wet, freshly turned soil, his eyes roll with excitement. Fuming up from his scrape, the siren-scent of a doe fully in estrus fires his blood. Nose to the ground, the buck locks onto the mind-blinding scent and takes up the trail in that stiff, short-gaited trot of rutting bucks.

The trail takes him into the cornfield and then on through a large fallow field. The buck gives little heed to the unfamiliar reality that he's in the broad open in full daylight. His mind is on one thing—the doe that left her calling card in his scrape. Unerringly, his nose takes him to her. Two small bucks have already found her. He rushes in and scatters them. He then turns to the doe, but though ready, she is teasingly unwilling to accept his advances. A chase ensues. The same scene is being played out throughout whitetail range. The first major wave of does has entered estrus and the breeding period has begun.

A day or two before a doe actually comes into estrus, she starts showing signs of its approach, urinating on her tarsal glands and emitting the telltale scent of coming heat. She may well begin seeking out a buck by visiting scrapes. Many experts even think that the alpha doe will seek out the dominant buck in the area. One thing is for certain, whether in a scrape, on her trail, or wafting along on a gentle forest breeze, her powerful scent will soon find its way to the nostrils of a lovesick buck. And in short order, he will find her. If he is able to fend off other bucks, he'll usually, but not always (I've seen several bucks breed the same doe), remain with her until she goes out of estrus, which only lasts 24 hours. Then, he'll head off in search of another receptive doe, revisiting doe groups or his scrapes—if he doesn't come across a hot doe right away.

When the first wave of does comes into heat, the normally ordered life of the whitetail deer turns to chaos. Predictable travel and movement patterns are a thing of the past. The bucks lower their defenses and can be so totally obsessed by the breeding urge that they appear plain stupid. The woods, and often the fields, are astir with chasing, trailing and other rites of the rut. They may move at any hour of the day and expose themselves in ways and places unthinkable outside the breeding period. Bucks, even mature ones, may blindly follow the harried does wherever they lead them, shadowing their every move.

Dominant bucks get first choice of the hot does. In lightly hunted populations with low buck/doe ratios and good buck age structures, the young and subdominant bucks spend much of their time watching from the sidelines. I've seen as many as a half-dozen subordinate bucks looking on longingly as the "big boy" feverishly guards his lady and fends off persistent advances from the lesser hopefuls. At times, it seems that the doe actually enjoys exasperating her suitor by trying to break free of his defenses. In such cases, the buck will often work the doe back into position exactly like a quarter horse works a cow. To avoid the competitive situation, bucks will frequently take control and drive the doe off to isolated spots, which accounts in part for some of the ridiculous places bucks are sometimes found during the breeding period.

Anytime you have a bunch of lovesick males and a few

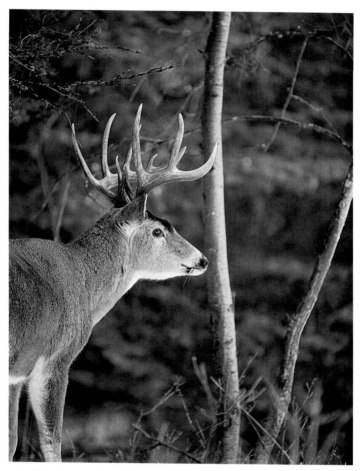

The breeding period is when bucks are the silliest, with even fully mature bucks seeming to throw caution to the winds. A problem is that movement tends to be random—but at least it's movement!

accommodating females, fights are sure to break out. This is certainly the case with bucks during the breeding period. The most serious fights of the year occur now when two dominant bucks lay claim to the same hot doe. Most fights are short and end in nothing more than damaged pride or chipped antlers, but occasionally, sex-driven battles are to the death.

Toward the end of the breeding period, the hectic pace begins to wane. The number of does in estrus declines, and the fervor of the bucks abates, their pent-up lust now partially satisfied. Gradually, the initial big wave of does passes through the first cycle and the breeding period draws to an end.

Hunting the Rut:

One of the best strategies during the breeding period is to spend as much time as you can hunting. Exposure alone swings the odds your way. The bucks will do a lot of the work for you since they're active and careless now. Aside from this, there are some specific things you can do to tilt the scales your way.

Strategy for the breeding period should begin with finding concentrations of deer. Where there are does, bucks are sure to be nearby. Two of the best places to start the search are major food sources and the staging areas associated with them. Look for evidence of heavy deer use, particularly rutting sign such as scrapes and rubs, scuff marks from buck fights, and running deer tracks made during chases. The presence of big rubs and scrapes, even if they are not well maintained, tells you that bucks use the area to hook up with does.

Rutting activity is sometimes concentrated in relatively localized pockets, perhaps because two or three does have come into estrus at the same time and drawn a crowd or simply because the area is the hub of local deer activity. Search out these places. Often, several bucks, and some-times even a couple of other does, will join in with a hot

Top-end bucks like this huge 10-pointer shot by the author in South Texas are most vulnerable during the rut. Hunters must take full advantage of this magical time.

doe to form a sizable breeding party. Breeding parties can leave considerable sign, especially in snow, and may hang in the same vicinity for two or three days. If you can locate such a party, you may be able to look over several bucks.

When I find a place with good general deer activity and encouraging buck sign, I adopt the hunting technique best suited to the situation. A hunter now has a wide range of options. Still-hunting, stand-hunting, deer drives, and even rattling can be successfully employed. However, when circumstances allow, my preferred hunting method—and the one that I believe can be the deadliest of all during the peak of rut—is what I call aggressive still-hunting. This method requires the right kind of country, plenty of room to roam and that the hunter possess considerable hunting skill.

The idea is to look over as much good habitat as possible at a pace that will allow you to see the deer before they see you. Certain conditions are best to accomplish this. First, the cover needs to be fairly open. If it is too thick, not only can't you look over much country, but worse, by the time you get close enough to the deer to see them, they will have probably already picked you off. Adequate distance tends to neutralize the deer's huge smell and hearing advantages. This makes the hunt more of a contest of sight, which a hunter has a chance of winning since he's alert and the buck may be distracted by thoughts of love. Generally, I consider less than 50 yards visibility to be too little for my still-hunting taste. I prefer at least 75 yards.

An ideal still-hunting area would also have routes through them that allow for quiet movement. Old logging roads, streambeds, firebreaks and the edges of fields, clearcuts and utility right-of-ways are likely prospects. Choose routes that provide some concealment and a diffused background. If possible, always look from thicker cover to thinner cover and from dark to light areas. Avoid a low sun in your face—not only can't you see but you will shine like a new penny. Hilly terrain offers the benefit of a concealed and silent approach as you peek over ridges, as well as the advantage of elevated views.

Still-hunting during the rut is an aggressive form of hunting. The hunter should move quietly but quickly through likely country, looking for prowling bucks or breeding parties. His mobility and the deer's lack of awareness allow the hunter to take liberties not normally possible. I've followed trailing bucks and had them lead me to breeding parties. Several times, I shadowed breeding parties for some distance to get a better look and/or a shot at bucks involved in the chase. I've killed bucks this way that would have escaped unscathed had I been immobile in a stand. And countless times, I've walked up on shootable bucks staring at me in a lovesick stupor that would have been long gone outside of the rut.

Rattling (and to a lesser degree, grunting) fits in perfectly with this active style of hunting and with the aggressive mood of the bucks during the breeding period. One of my favorite strategies is to walk, stop, and rattle all day long. I generally rattle with lots of enthusiasm during the peak of rut, starting out with brush-rubbing and limb-breaking, moving into knuckle-cracking antler-rattling and ending with some serious ground-stomping using the butt of the horns. Then, I wrap the whole sequence up with two or three grunts. (In my opinion, a grunt call is at its best when used in conjunction with rattling.) I'll wait about three to five minutes, grunt again a couple of times, wait another minute and then either start the sequence over again or leave for another place.

I'll often use rattling and grunting during the rut as a ploy to make a buck stop, look my way or to show himself with no intention of calling him in. This can be especially useful for making an unseen or unidentified buck move into view when looking over an area with enough cover to conceal a buck but not enough to completely block your sight.

During the rut, the still-hunter has extreme flexibility and can adapt to any new circumstance. He can change his course to accommodate a shift in wind or to take advantage of a ridge that offers a good view of promising country. If a buck is spooked, the hunter can try a quick maneuver to cut him off or loop around him. Upon finding hot sign or seeing a suspicious-acting deer, he may choose to shift to a stop-and-go hunt moving at a snail's pace or perhaps sit for a while at the base of a convenient tree. In snow conditions, he may pick up fresh tracks and follow them. Still-hunting during the peak of rut is a wide open field . . . and hunting in its purest form!

If thick cover, small land tract size, or noisy conditions

During the peak of the rut, bucks are sometimes caught in places no self-respecting trophy buck would ever be—like in the middle of a bald-open field!

prevent still-hunting, my second choice is stand-hunting. I try to set up where I can look over as much good deer country as possible to take advantage of the high level of movement and the fact that bucks aren't as hesitant now to leave the security of thick cover. Relatively open hardwood bottoms, clearcuts, especially those with some cover, isolated openings, and fallow fields are all possible ambush points. The stand site should, of course, be located in high-activity areas with buck signs or on major travel corridors. If possible, I like to locate in bottlenecks that physically funnel activity and cutlines.

Deer drives work very well during the breeding period. When deer are on their feet and moving, they are far easier to drive than bedded deer. Plus, mature bucks normally don't drive very well; they prefer instead to sneak and circle or to hold tight in cover. Now these same bucks may follow the does into more vulnerable situations than they would choose of their own accord. Drives are particularly effective in the snow because of the great advantage snow affords in reading sign and tracking. In areas with limited or broken cover, such as the Midwest, Central Canada and the Great Plains, a handful of experienced hunters aided by fresh snow can drive deer with deadly effectiveness.

As we said earlier, rattling works during the breeding period, though results can be unpredictable. Some hunters believe that the most likely respondents will be young or subdominant bucks. The logic is that the more dominant bucks will be with does and that they are seldom willing to abandon a hot doe to traipse off to a fight. I agree with this only in part. The truth is that trophy bucks often can be rattled in during the breeding period. There are some simple reasons for this. First, there's always the chance of catching a trophy buck between does that might want to look in on a fight. Second, dominance is not always based on antler size, and it is very possible that a subdominant buck will qualify as a trophy. Several times I've watched fights where the better buck (based on rack size) was defeated by a bigger-bodied but smaller-racked buck. Finally, anything can happen during the breeding period!

CHAPTER TEN

THE POST-RUT PERIOD

I've tried hard to find a way around it, but I regretfully must admit that the post-rut period is the most difficult time to hunt trophy whitetails, especially if they're subjected to much hunting pressure. They are now perfectly content to while away their daylight hours in the security of thick cover if bothered by man. In fact, even if not disturbed, older bucks are going to be largely nocturnal during this time.

The post-rut is a somewhat complex period and can be divided into three different stages based on behavioral patterns. The first is what I call the "waning rut." This stage includes both the tail-off breeding activity immediately following the peak breeding period and the relatively minor secondary rut. The greatest activity of the waning rut occurs during the first three to four weeks of the post-rut period. These last flurries of breeding activity probably represent the best chance a hunter has for a trophy during the post-rut period.

The second stage is what I call the "post-rut lull," and for good reason: bucks lay low in thick cover and recuperate from the rigors of the rut during this time. They can seem to virtually disappear from the face of the Earth during this stage.

The third and last stage occurs when the bucks return to a feeding pattern. Prospects brighten somewhat now, depending on hunting pressure, the availability of prime food sources, herd density and the severity of the winter. Before looking at these three stages, let's explore the timing and length of the post-rut period.

TIMING AND DURATION

The post-rut period starts when the two-week breeding period ends. Therefore, the timing of the post-rut period can be determined by adding two weeks to the starting date of the breeding period, the key to timing all four periods of fall deer activity. The beginning of the post-rut period is marked by a dramatic decline in breeding activity, though remnant breeding does continue for a while as we've discussed.

The close of the post-rut is brought about by a specific event: antler-shedding. When bucks drop their antlers can vary greatly from place to place and can even vary somewhat from year to year within the same place. Obviously, when peak rut occurs is the key factor affecting place to place timing, but the condition of the bucks contributes to year to year variances at a given locale. Generally, the better the bucks' condition, or put another way, the less stressed, the later they drop their antlers.

The most prevalent time throughout the country for antler-shedding is January through mid-February. Montana whitetails, for instance, have pretty much lost their antlers by mid-January. However, South Texas bucks drop their antlers much later, in March and even early April. Bucks in Alabama, where the rut is very late, don't normally lose their antlers until March. Frankly, when the post-rut ends and exactly how long it lasts are of little concern to hunters since few places have hunting seasons extending to the end of the period.

THE WANING RUT

As the peak rut comes to an end, breeding and its related activities begin to wind down. With fewer does in heat, the general chaos eases. During the first couple of weeks, breeding activity is dependent upon the late arrivals to estrus, the number of which diminishes steadily as time passes. Still, the bucks are hopeful and remain focused primarily on breeding. When the bucks start having trouble picking up hot does, they range out looking for receptive does, anxiously checking the doe groups. Their travel pattern is somewhat like that of the scraping period, only less predictable, more nocturnal and accompanied by much less sign-making. They are now looking directly for a willing doe and depend on their noses to reveal her presence.

About two weeks into the post-rut period, the dwindling breeding activity can get a shot in the arm by the arrival of the secondary rut. If this second cycle, made up mostly of 1½- year-old does, is significant, the breeding ritual is again played out on a mini-scale. Overall activity is, however, far less widespread. Much of the limited breeding activity takes place at night, the cumulative results of growing weariness and ongoing hunting pressure. From the hunter's perspective, visible rutting activity will be isolated and sporadic and fresh buck sign will be sparse.

About a month into the period, the waning rut is pretty much over. With each passing day that a buck doesn't score, his enthusiasm wanes. Gradually, rutting activity gives way to resting or brief periods of feeding. The buck's travels become less extensive. Doe groups drop off his route. The buck soon drifts back to his core area and starts passing the daylight hours bedded in his familiar territory. Slowly, the urge to breed loses its grip on him and the need to rest and recover from the rigors of the rut takes priority. Only the alluring scent of a hot doe can rekindle the fire in a rut-weary buck. Maybe it's an isolated late doe that comes into estrus and rearranges his schedule. Or, perhaps it's the minor third cycle, which usually hits about six weeks into the post-rut period and consists mostly of six-month-old doe fawns, that brings that familiar, all-powerful scent back to the deer woods. Even then, the effects are limited and short-lived.

THE POST-RUT LULL

As the power of the rut relaxes its hold, the post-rut lull sets in. Deer begin the shift to a quieter, more settled lifestyle. Cold, plus rain and/or snow, have reduced the amount of secure cover available to deer. The leaves have fallen off the trees, the underbrush has been denuded and the tall grass is laid low. The food supply, once fairly well distributed over much of the deer's range, is now diminished both in quantity and distribution. The deer, haggard and skittish, feel the stress and fatigue brought on by the frantic pace of the previous weeks. Their priority now becomes rest and food. They seek refuge in the remaining pockets of thick, secure cover and devote evermore time and attention to nourishing their neglected bodies.

Does, fawns, and young bucks come through the rut in fairly good shape physically and quickly return to something resembling a regular feeding pattern, perhaps bedding in thick pockets of cover near the food source

After the rut bucks often simply disappear, resting, recuperating and licking their wounds in the deepest thickets.

during the day and feeding at first and last light and at night. Hunting pressure will determine the level of daytime activity.

With mature bucks, the routine immediately following the last days of significant breeding is different. Having neglected both food and rest, they now find themselves exhausted. For a time, their drive to feed takes a back seat to their desire for rest and solitude. The older bucks, already back in their core area, seek out the thickest or most secure areas to bed. Their privacy and rest assured, they will feed some, but mostly at night and near their beds. As far as the hunter is concerned, mature bucks often seem to cease to exist in the midst of the post-rut lull.

It's hard to say how long the lull lasts. Remnant breeding activity tends to override and confuse the pattern, as does hunting pressure. Movement and sign are so limited that figuring out exactly what deer are doing is difficult. The severity of the climate (the cold), the physical condition of the deer and, of course, hunting pressure are all factors in how long it takes adult bucks to return to a consistent feeding pattern. My guess is that this recuperation time usually lasts from one to two weeks before giving way to a consistent feeding pattern.

FEEDING AGAIN

In time, rut-weary bucks slowly regain their strength by resting long hours and feeding on food sources convenient to their bedding areas. Winter is upon them, and the bucks feel the need to nourish themselves in preparation for the hard times ahead. Gradually, their daily routine shifts. They venture out farther and farther from their core areas in search of quality food. If preferred agricultural crops are in the area, you can be sure that most bucks eventually will end up feeding there. Clearcuts and other concentrated food sources will also draw their attention. In the absence of concentrated feed, the deer scatter over the entire range and forage as best they can. The feeding pattern now is much like that of the pre-rut period except that the bucks are more nocturnal, food sources are fewer and more localized, and the deer may have to travel even farther for prime feed. The hunting prospects during this time depend

Jennifer Morris shot this fine Montana eight-pointer early into the post-rut period, during the "waning rut," probably the best post-rut period to take a buck.

largely on the presence of major food sources to concentrate deer and on hunting pressure.

Concentrations of deer can be phenomenal during the late post-rut, especially in the cold latitudes and overcrowded populations. (Fortunately for the deer, hunting season is seldom in when these concentrations occur.) I've seen situations where deer from miles around seem to converge on a major food source. Their quest for food may even cause them to abandon their core areas for a time and relocate miles away near prime food sources. An extreme example of this is the actual whitetail migrations that take place in the mountainous regions of the West.

Severe winter weather and deep snows also can cause deer in harsh northern climates to concentrate in the limited protective cover. This is called "yarding." We won't focus on yarding per se since deer are seldom hunted at such times. I mention it because this extreme behavior is somewhat indicative of what deer across the country do in the late post-rut period. They will bunch up in the best available cover, although to a far less exaggerated degree than in classic yarding. In middle Georgia, for instance, deer "herd up" in pockets of thick evergreens in impressive numbers after winter has "burned" the cover back. They spend most of their time in these protective pockets of cover, venturing out only to feed. I've seen this same situation everywhere I've hunted, except in places such as South Texas, Florida, and the coastal "jungles" of the South where widespread cover is maintained even during the winter. This tendency toward yarding during the post-rut period creates an ideal situation for driving deer. The only problem is that trophy bucks aren't always bedded with the large concentrations of deer found in the obvious pockets of cover.

HUNTING THE POST-RUT

Hunting the post-rut is not an enviable task, especially when trophy bucks are the goal. Where pressure is high, the deer probably have been shot at, run off their feeding grounds, kept awake during their daily nap times and even disturbed on "hot dates." Under such conditions, even does, fawns, and young bucks will resort almost totally to nocturnal sorties and you certainly won't find mature bucks up and about of their own accord in the daylight. The more pressure, the more reclusive and nocturnal the deer become and the longer it takes them to return to normal activity.

During the first three to four weeks of the post-rut, the best game in town is the low-level rutting activity brought on by latecomers from the first breeding cycle and by the secondary rut. The strategy is about the same

During the post-rut period, survival becomes a significant concern for rut-weary bucks. Especially in northern areas, the onset of winter catches bucks at their worst physical condition.

as for the breeding period— hunt the doe concentrations, preferably those where big buck sign can be found, even if it's not too fresh. Unfortunately, bucks don't leave much sign during the post-rut. The best evidence of rutting activity is to actually see a buck trailing or chasing. If you see this, hunt the area hard. There could be several bucks, including the local "big cheese," working the vicinity in hopes of connecting with one of the relatively few does now in heat.

If I believe a hot doe is in the area, I prefer to slip quietly through the woods in search of the breeding party. Stand-hunting is better if no rutting activity is evident since deer are very skittish now. Rattling can work during the waning rut, but results will be spotty. In fact, I've actually seen bucks run from rattling during the post-rut. On the other hand, I've had some success by rattling rather modestly in one spot and then waiting patiently for long periods, which for me is 20 to 30 minutes. Unless a hot doe is around to fire the bucks up, I've found that post-rut bucks respond very cautiously and usually prefer to scent-check some distance downwind rather than approach the fake fight directly as they might earlier.

If forced movement is ever the best way to hunt trophy whitetails, it is during the post-rut lull. I employ two different hunting tactics to force movement during this time. One, I slip ever so slowly through thickets that are likely big buck bedding areas. Three good things can come from this. I may jump a buck and get a quick shot. A buck may stand up and hold momentarily for a shot upon hearing a slight noise or seeing an unidentifiable movement. Or, I may catch an unsuspecting buck loitering around in his bedding area. Of course, a number of bad things can happen, and they considerably outweigh the good. That aside, I have killed a couple of trophy bucks using this rather desperate tactic. However, I confess my return on investment is meager when invading a buck's bedding area.

The other tactic to force movement is deer drives. There is no other time of year when deer drives are as justified. There are times and situations during the post-rut period when deer simply won't move unless you move them. The success of deer drives now depends on knowing where big bucks might be bedded.

The post-rut lull is the time for what I call "micro-hunting." Let me explain. During the scraping and breeding periods particularly, bucks are on the move and can cover lots of country, sometimes even exposing themselves in the relative open during full daylight. It is generally to the hunter's advantage during such times to look over as much deer habitat as possible. Not so after the tail-off breeding has wound down and the lull has set in. During this time, mature bucks don't move much or travel far in the daytime and what movement there is normally takes place in thick cover. This forces the hunter to focus on thick-cover sanctuaries and pinpoint a specific spot to ambush a buck within the relatively small area he's likely to be moving about in. This is micro-hunting and, to be honest, it's not my cup of tea. You can see why I said earlier that the best bet is to take advantage of the remnant breeding activity early in the period.

Hunting in close quarters leaves no room for mistakes. A favorable wind and total quiet are essential. I'll often take a seat next to a sizable tree rather than risk making noise while hanging a stand. Hunting like this is slow and tedious. But if you want to shoot a big buck now, hunting them where they are— in the thickets—is not a bad idea. As always, don't pick a stand site randomly. Find some sort of sign that says a good buck is frequenting the area.

When mature bucks settle into a feeding pattern during the post-rut period, a hunter's options increase, assuming

Late in the post-rut period, bucks, haggard and tired from the rigors of the rut, return to a feeding pattern. In most areas, the deer season is over before this occurs.

deer season is still open, which is seldom the case. The hunting strategy called for is essentially the same employed during the pre-rut period. In pressured areas, emphasis should be placed on hunting the staging grounds near major food sources or trails leading to and from bedding/feeding areas. As a general rule, the higher the pressure, the closer to the bedding area and the denser the cover you'll need to hunt. Conversely, the lower the pressure, the closer to the food source you should hunt. In very low pressure situations, even hunting open food sources may be productive.

Considerable scouting may be needed during the post-rut period to find the best place to wait out a buck headed to food. Stand-hunting is the most reliable way to hunt bucks on a feeding pattern. Still-hunting can also be effective if conditions are right, but deer are spooky now and difficult to sneak up on. Hunt to the last legal minute of the day and be in position in the morning before first light. Try to find bottlenecks or some physical feature to help funnel a buck your way. Even if you do everything right, you'll still need a large dose of patience and a double dose of luck to kill a big buck during the post-rut!

CHAPTER ELEVEN

CLOSING THOUGHTS

As you have gathered by now, the emphasis of this book is on hunting where trophy bucks live and knowing enough about whitetail movement patterns to be able to predict what trophy bucks are likely to be doing before ever stepping foot in the woods. As we wrap up, let's again put these two elements in perspective.

If your aim is to shoot a trophy buck, the most important step you can take toward success is to search out and hunt places that have appreciable numbers of what you're looking for. This is the very foundation of consistent success, and if you build your deer hunting strategy on any foundation other than that, you will be destined to failure. It's an inescapable fact that nobody can kill something that's not there. Skill, experience, hunting tactics, perseverance, and even luck only become factors in success if what you're after is actually walking around out there. Even then, you still may not kill your trophy, but if you don't hunt where he lives, I guarantee you won't!

The second emphasis in this book is on patterning trophy bucks, especially in relation to the movement and travel patterns before, during, and after the all-important rut. Buck behavior and travel during the fall follow predictable big-picture patterns that are so dependably repeated from year to year that you can actually know in advance what trophy bucks are likely to be doing at a given time under a given set of circumstances. That's the beauty of understanding the basic biology of the animal and his behavioral patterns—you can hunt anywhere, anytime and, after doing some onsite homework, closely predict what the deer are likely to be doing, where they're doing it, and what tactics will work. Aside from the "where factor," I don't know what could be more important to success than this.

Now, one final note. This book has focused on hunting trophy bucks. We've defined a trophy buck according to the objective perspective of the total universe of deer hunters— namely, a trophy is a mature buck, at least 3½ years old, that is among the largest consistently taken in an area. That leaves room for place-to-place size differences and even some latitude for case-by-case judgement calls as to what is and is not a trophy. But frankly, when it gets right down to it, I still like the subjective individual definition that says "a trophy is a prized memento of one's personal accomplishment." You see, I do believe "trophy" is in the eyes of the beholder. If a hunter is proud of his buck, regardless of the size, nobody has the right to say that deer is not a trophy.

I have become sensitive to this in recent years as trophy hunting has increased in popularity and the term "trophy" has become more synonymous with "really big." As a result, a type of trophy snobbery has crept into our ranks. If a buck doesn't meet the standards of the trophy snob, both the hunter and his game are belittled—perhaps in mean-spirited terms or more often in subtle, condescending ways. Regardless of how, it's wrong, and I believe it is detrimental to the sport since it tends to especially discourage and even demoralize the young and inexperienced, who must eventually carry the hunting banner.

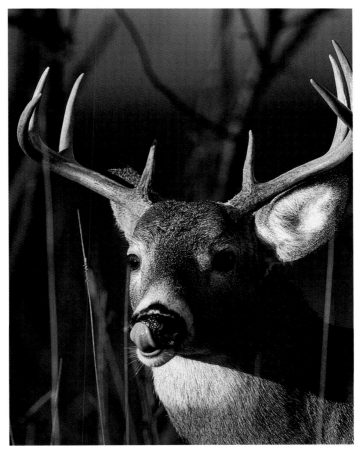

Antlers are not only beautiful but give hunters a yardstick for judging quality. However, it's really the whitetail's keen senses—eyes, ears, and nose—that make him the great trophy he is.

And in case you haven't looked around lately, we hunters need all the folks we can get to line up on our side.

This issue is fresh on my mind because I just saw a textbook case played out. I was speaking to kids in the local school about, of all things, whitetail hunting (only in Montana!), and I asked who had taken a deer the past season. Several hands went up. Then I asked, foolishly perhaps, if anyone had killed a trophy. One 12-year-old kid I knew well raised his hand high; in fact, he practically came out of his seat, a smile etched across his face. "I did! I did!" he shouted.

An adult, who prided himself on being an accomplished trophy hunter, responded in a patronizing voice, "Sit down, Joe. Your buck was just a nice eight-pointer, not a trophy."

I felt ashamed of asking the question and, in a way, of being a trophy hunter. I remembered the unbridled pride I had when I shot my first buck, which wasn't nearly as big as Joe's, and I thought about how I would have felt if someone had told me he wasn't a trophy. I walked over to Joe, who looked completely deflated, and as I gave him a 'high five,' I said, "Congratulations on a great trophy! It took me 10 years of hard hunting to kill a buck like yours."

Joe beamed with pride. So did I!

INDEX

Note: Bold page numbers indicate illustrations or photos.

acorns, 88, 89
activity. *See* movement
age, buck
   of maturity, 8–9, 18,
      23–25
   structure, 21–23, 26
   vulnerability and, 10–13
Alabama, 49
antler(s)
   hard, 77, 83
   nutrition effect on, 20
   rattling, 30–31
      breeding period, 123,
         125, 127
      post-rut, 138
      pre-rut, 96
      scraping period,
         100–101, 111,
         112–13

shedding, 83, 130

bedding areas
   post-rut, 132–34
   pre-rut, 90–93
Boland, Dave, 44
Boone & Crockett records,
      43–51, **45–46**
   Canada, central, 69–71,
      69
   Canada, eastern, 71–72,
      69
   East, 55–57, **56**
   hunting pressure effect
      on, **36, 38, 39**
   Mexico, 20, 68–69, 68
   Midwest, 60–61, **60**
   North region, 54–55, **54**

Northwest, 63–64, **63**
Plains & Prairies, 62–63, **62**
South, 57–59, **57**
Southwest, 64–68, **65**
boots, 111
breeding period, 115–17
  hunting, 122–27
  movement, 119–27
  timing and length, 117–19
  See also rut
buck
  aggression of, 83–84, 101, 106, 121–22
  buck/doe ratio, 20–21, 26–27, 34–35
  mature, 8–9, 18–19
  survival instincts, 10–13
  trophy, 8–9, 13, 18–19, 144
Burnt Pine Plantation, 10

calling, grunt, 111, 125
Canada, 20, 91
  central, 69–71, **71**
  eastern, 71–72, **71**
  records, 44, 49, 55, 63–64, **63**

Connecticut, 56
cover scent, 111

doe(s)
  alpha, 93, 119
  buck/doe ratio, 20–21, 26–27, 34–35
  estrus, 105–7, 117–18, 119–20
  groups, 84, 93–94
  pre-rut, 84, 85
  scrapes, 104
drives, deer
  breeding period, 123, 126–27
  post-rut, 138–39
  pre-rut, 96
  scraping period, 112

Eufaula, Lake, 15
estrus, 105–7, 117–18, 119–20

fawns, 20–21
  in tertiary rut, 117–18, 132
feeding areas

post-rut, 134–36
pre-rut, 88–90, 92–93
flehemening, 106

genetics, 23–24, 37–38,
    38, 48
Georgia, 38–41, *39,* 48
glands
    preorbital, 103
    tarsal, 103, 104, 119
grunt calling, 111, 125

habitat, 27
    See also regions
Hanson, Milo, 49
hunting
    difficulty, 13, 25–27.
        See also under specific
        region
    micro-, 139
    post-rut, 129, 136–41
    pre-rut, 94–96
    rut, 122–27
    scrape, 107–13

Idaho, 48
Illinois, 48

Indiana, 48, 49, 51
Iowa, 47–48, 51

Jacobson's organ, 106

Kansas, 48, 51
Kentucky, 48, 49

land, hunting, 25
    See also regions

Maine, 55
maps, topographical, 94
Maryland, 56
Massachusetts, 56
Mexico, 20, 68–69, **68**
Michigan, 48, 55
Minnesota, 44, 47–48, 51,
    55
Mississippi, 44
Missouri, 48
Montana, 38–41, **39,** 48
moon, phases of, 25
Morris, Jennifer, **135**
movement
    breeding period, 119–22

forced, 138–39
hunting pressure effect
    on, 26–27, 34–35
post-rut, 131–36,
    138–39
pre-rut, 84
scraping period, 105–7
seasonal, 75–80, **77**
See also drives, deer

Nebraska, 48
New Hampshire, 55, 56
New Jersey, 56
New York, 55
nutrition, 20, 23–24,
    37–38, **38**

Ohio, 48, 51

Pennsylvania, 56
photographs, aerial, 94
photoperiodism, 75
population, 16–19, 43
  age structure of, 21–23,
    26
  buck/doe ratio, 20–21

herd density, 19–20, 25
hunting pressure effect
    on, 32–41, **36, 38, 39**
North America
  Canada, central,
    69–71, **69**
  Canada, eastern,
    71–72, **71**
  East, 55–57, **56**
  Mexico, 20, 68–69, **68**
  Midwest, 60–61, **60**
  North region, 54–55,
    54
  Northwest, 63–64, **63**
  Plains & Prairies,
    62–63, **62**
  South, 57–59, **57**
  Southwest, 64–68, **65**
post-rut
  hunting, 129, 136–41
  lull, 129, 132–34
  movement, 131–36
  timing and length,
    130–31
  waning rut, 129, 131–32
  yarding, 135–36
pre-rut
  bedding, 90–93
  feeding, 88–90, 92–93

hunting, 94–96
hunting pressure, 95
sign, 84–88
pressure, hunting
  age structure and,
    21–23, 26
  breeding period, 118–19
  buck/doe ratio and,
    20–21, 34–35
  levels of, 33–35
  movement and, 26–27,
    34–35
  population and, 32–41,
    36, 38, 39
  pre-rut, 95
  records and, 44
  regional. *See* specific
    region
  scrapes and, 109–10
  sign and, 34–35
  size and, 23–25, 35–37

rattling, antler, 30–31
  breeding period, 123,
    125, 127
  post-rut, 138
  pre-rut, 96
  scraping period,
    100–101, 111, 112–13

records, Boone & Crockett,
  43–51, **45–46**
  hunting pressure effect
    on, **36, 38, 39**
  See also specific region
Records of North America
  Big Game (B&C), 44
regions
  Canada, central, 69–71,
    69
  Canada, eastern, 71–72, **71**
  East, 55–57, **56**
  Mexico, 20, 68–69, **68**
  Midwest, 60–61, **60**
  North region, 54–55, **54**
  Northwest, 63–64, **63**
  Plains & Prairies, 62–63,
    62
  South, 57–59, **57**
  Southwest, 64–68, **65**
Rhode Island, 56
rub(s)
  breeding, 103–4
  pre-rut, 84–87, 89–90,
    92–93
  rubline, 103
  scraping period, 102–5,
    110
  signpost, 86–87
  size, 85, 87, 105

rut
    hunting pressure during,
        26–27, 34–35
    peak of, 117, 118
    periods of, 76–77
        breeding, 78–79,
        115–27
        post-rut, 80, 129–41
        pre-rut, 77–78, 83–96
        scraping, 78, 99–113
    secondary, 117–18, 131
    tertiary, 117–18, 132

scores. *See* records, Boone
    & Crockett
scrape(s)
    boundary, 87
    doe, 104
    hunting, 107–13
    hunting pressure and,
        109–10
    pre-rut, 84–87
    scouting, 109–10
    scrapeline, 103
    in scraping period,
        102–5
    size of, 105
    trail, 87

scraping period
    hunting, 107–13
    movement, 105–7
    sign of, 102–5, 110
    timing and length, 101–2
season, hunting, 25
Shanks, Guy, **109**
sign
    hunting pressure and,
        34–35
    post-rut, 134, 137–38
    pre-rut, 84–88, 89–90
    scraping period, 102–5,
        110
size, buck
    factors in, 23–25
    hunting pressure effect
        on, 23–25, 35–41, **36,
        38, 39**
    regional, 23, 37–41, **38,
        39**
    rubs and, 85, 87
    scrapes and, 105
    tracks and, 87–88
    See also records, Boone &
        Crockett
Spears, Steve, **112**
stand-hunting
    post-rut, 138, 140

pre-rut, 96
rut, 123, 126
scrape, 110, 111–12
still-hunting
   aggressive, 123–26
   post-rut, 140
   pre-rut, 96
   rut, 123–26
subspecies, 23, 37

terrain, 27
   See also specific region
testosterone, 85, 101
Texas, 48, 51, 64–68, **65**
tracks, 87–88
trails, connecting
   pre-rut, 92–93
   rubs, 89–90
   scraping area, 110

Vermont, 55, 56

Virginia, 49

Washington, 48

weather, 25, 91, 135–36

West Virginia, 56

Wisconsin, 44, 47, 55

yarding, 135–36

PHOTOGRAPHY CREDITS

Mark Raycroft: Opposite Table of Contents, 9, 47, 137, 145

Charles Alsheimer: 14, 28, 42, 52, 74, 82, 98, 114, 128, 142

David Morris: 17, 31, 32, 50, 73, 76, 109, 112, 116, 123, 126, 135, 140

John Ford: 22, 79, 133

Bill Kinney: 40, 89

Grady Allen: 58, cover

Ian McMurchy: 61, 81, 121

Lon E. Lauber: 86

Lance Krueger: 97